THE COMPLEXITIES
of INTIMACY

THE
COMPLEXITIES
of INTIMACY

STORIES BY

MARY CAPONEGRO

COFFEE HOUSE PRESS

2001

COFFEE HOUSE PRESS is an independent nonprofit literary publisher supported in part by a grant provided by the Minnesota State Arts Board, through an appropriation by the Minnesota State Legislature, and in part by a grant from the National Endowment for the Arts. Significant support was received for this project through a grant from the National Endowment for the Arts, a federal agency. Support has also been provided by Athwin Foundation; the Bush Foundation; Buuck Family Foundation; Elmer L. & Eleanor J. Andersen Foundation; Honeywell Foundation; James R. Thorpe Foundation; Lila Wallace-Reader's Digest Fund; McKnight Foundation; Patrick and Aimee Butler Family Foundation; The St. Paul Companies Foundation, Inc.; the law firm of Schwegman, Lundberg, Woessner & Kluth, P.A.; Star Tribune Foundation; the Target Foundation; Wells Fargo Foundation Minnesota; West Group; and many individual donors. To you and our many readers across the country, we send our thanks for your continuing support.

COFFEE HOUSE PRESS books are available to the trade through our primary distributor, Consortium Book Sales & Distribution, 1045 Westgate Drive, Saint Paul, MN 55114. For personal orders, catalogs, or other information, write to: Coffee House Press, 27 North Fourth Street, Suite 400, Minneapolis, MN 55401.

LIBRARY OF CONGRESS CIP INFORMATION
Caponegro, Mary, 1956-
    The complexities of intimacy : stories / by Mary Caponegro.
        p. cm.
    ISBN 1-56689-120-5 (alk. paper)
    1. Domestic fiction, American.   I. Title.
PS3553.A5877 C66 2001
813'.54--DC21

                                                    2001032482

10 9 8 7 6 5 4 3 2 1
FIRST EDITION / FIRST PRINTING
PRINTED IN CANADA

The following stories appeared in literary magazines in slightly different form: "The Daughter's Lamentation," under the title "The Complexities of Intimacy," in *Conjunctions,* "The Mother's Mirror," under the title "The Further Complexities of Intimacy," also in *Conjunctions,* "The Father's Blessing," under the title "The Priest's Tale," in *Sulfur,* "Epilogue of the Progeny," under the title "Whoever Is Never Born with the Most Toys Wins," in *Gargoyle,* and the novella, "The Son's Burden," in *Epoch.*

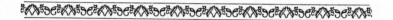

CONTENTS

for Michael

THE DAUGHTER'S LAMENTATION

While I was growing up, my family maintained a house in the northwestern part of the state, on the largest of the bodies of water known as the Finger Lakes. It was intended principally as a summer residence, and occasionally it even served this function, but more often it was rented out to strangers because my father liked to travel a good deal; you might say he had a passion for it. Moreover, he wanted his family to participate in his passion, and so we dutifully accompanied him, regardless of our inclinations. My sisters gradually became disaffected with this lifestyle, and with the one who imposed it upon them; my mother became exhausted; in fact, extinguished: though younger than my father by some years, she passed away well before him.

I remain today the only loyal sibling, unable, either through an excess of nobility or stupidity, to surrender the filial piety that binds me even now to this house, this past, this in every sense singular parent, my father, who, it seems, after so many years of nearly nomadic existence, has finally cultivated a yen for stasis, contemplation, and has chosen to occupy in his retirement the house in which I cannot honestly say I was raised. I often think some horizontal metaphor would be more accurately descriptive of the widely disseminated influences of my formative years. This is, however, the house in which I might have grown up, and it strangely elicits—albeit elliptically—an even greater poignancy.

It is customary, is it not, in times of loss or instability, to cultivate an intimacy with memories? In these instances, we tend to create structures that reinforce familiarity, but with my father this is not the case; he seems in fact quite awkward with the consequences of what he has created, or adopted. He claims that the particular shape of this wooden box, the angle at which it meets the earth, the vast window that looks onto the lake: these things create in the house an odd emotion, and thus create for him disconcerting sensations. I too am somewhat sensitive to ambience and want to ease his awkwardness if I've the means to do so.

For instance, I have offered to support the less-than-solid foundation, like Atlas supporting the world. True, I possess more stamina than strength, and the grand rhetoric of generosity is largely gesture. But on a more pragmatic plane, I also offer regularly to paint, to caulk, to scrape or spackle, sweep or scrub— but no, he says I must not trouble; besides, it is obvious that these cosmetic imperfections are but symptoms of the monumental underlying problems that beset the modest-appearing structure. Might I then catch the door before it makes the sound he cares so little for, offer an appendage as a hinge of sorts? I'd stay the door with hand or foot before it had a chance to slam, for many years of ballet are behind me; all of his children were trained in one or another of the arts, and the grace I learned is evident only

MARY CAPONEGRO

in the most humble circumstance: standing waiting for a train, for instance, note my posture, bearing, the drama of my silhouette as I lean against a pillar just outside the station. This quality is often commented upon by strangers, though never by my father, who takes grace—at least mine—for granted. There are worse sins, I tell my sisters, who harp on his neglect, than overlooking admirable attributes. Those closest to us often are the most blind. It does not really constitute transgression.

The house, however, is another matter, conforming to no law with which I am acquainted: a kind of wood box slightly skew; not salt box, neither hat nor shoe, a leaning tower without a Pisa's dignity, haphazard, squat, and deep within, a strange conglomerate of spaces extending from cellar to attic, each appearing infinite, made separate instead of connected by series of steps, altogether unfinished yet cramped. He would finish the basement, he always said, so my sisters and I could play, and also the attic, to use as his study, but we were as family too transient to allow feasibility of any long-term project—still less likely now to be considered by him who communes incessantly with infinity.

He seems to revel in or be resigned, at any rate, to the rawness of the space. Nearly one entire wall is glass, and the body of water, viewed through the former's transparency, often gives the appearance of glass, and across the former, my father, in a perplexingly unamphibious manner, swims: propels himself against its smooth surface, and I follow him anxiously (as if he were child and I powerless but nonetheless protective parent), utterly transfixed by his trajectory, for I have no notion whatsoever why he does not fall. Fortunately no one passes outside—for no one ever visits—because it might be shocking to behold the manner in which his arms and legs work the surface as if he were another sort of creature entirely, lacking only wings, or were performing some very private—indeed, primordial—function publicly, groping with the body as if his entire corpus were undifferentiated as separate trunk and limbs.

Etiquette would not permit my asking if he built the house himself; I know I should know, it should be obvious, from his remarks and its marked features. Who am I to say (having been born last, the youngest of my sisters)? It certainly bears the stamp of his originality. "It's vision I uphold, not roof and walls," I can recall his saying, bellowing from his pulpit/drafting table. Later in his life he ceased to plan, declaring mutiny from his profession, accusing it of treachery: "Should I then bracket all my dreams and only build to code, to code, to code?" Indeed, I find it hard to picture saw or hammer in his hand.

Perhaps he only designed the house and others carried out his vision: something lost, as the expression goes, in translation. It may be merely inept execution then, and yet it feels like destiny. In any case, the toll it takes upon him is significant; his delicacy, in truth not less than mine, and perhaps greater, as I have trained my body to withstand stress, and endure, to some extent, the elements. For instance, many times I have remarked that living at the water invites cold and damp into his house and bones; thus proper insulation is imperative—so much glass and ample draft—if not possible for the building then the occupant, in sufficent clothes—one must make a barrier lest harm should enter—and exercise the remedy for every ill and all imbalances from lethargy to nervousness, sciatica or hypertension, obesity, depression or distraction; I know how many prophylactic measures must be taken to insure against arthritis and the like, for once I entertained the fantasy of ballet as vocation (though now it seems absurd), enacting over and over on a stage the most stylized of romances—ironic that a sequence of steps and positions take nearly a lifetime to prepare and yield at best a stilted corporeal narrative—one is always leaping up from or into the arms of a man whose sex is trapped in a stocking, like the squeezed face of a thief: to make one pair of mobile mannequins, layered in gauze to render us weightless, lighter than air as we rise (in defiance of gravity), invisible buildings described by our bodies, rarely remaining for more than a moment. Are we not regal? Aren't we refined? And yet, how little different from a spider or a penguin or a crab: to move sideways across a stage with some stiff halo or sheer veil around my hips, while making gestures as if signaling a train, or tolling time with human hands; a fleshly cuckoo clock made mute, as I sport some ludicrous tiara on my head—ever my father's princess, my King, my Lear, whose suffering I see and feel, and make, against my will, my own; my maker, my betrayer; why can't I abandon you, abuser?

The house appears very small if viewed from outside—(as it scarcely ever is), but my clever father built, or had built—only he, I'm sure, could have designed—the peculiarly expansive contours, disconcerting though they are to experience, his iconoclastic brilliance apparent in every rafter, every pillar; space above and space below are unfathomably conflated; attic and cellar seem to converge such that it is easier to find oneself in the nether reaches of the house than in the house's body, if you will; it's like living in a trompe l'oeil painting cast in three dimensions. Somehow I always miss the middle, always one off from the ground floor, I am up, I'm down, I've never quite arrived, not unlike the sensation of leaping up from or into the arms of a man whose sex is trapped in a stocking—never resting, never stationary, my feet perpetually between steps; it keeps me, you might say, up on my toes, to be ascending or descending and whenever I'm at an end point I'm confused. I find the bulk of time is spent in transit, or lost among the clutter of centuries that, out of context, disorient me against my will, until I am able to achieve again the center of the house, where he gazes into the view, elemental and immense, water as hypnotic as fire. Sometimes I think he is building cities in the sea, the patterns made by light perceived as ligaments of vast imagined structures. Occasionally he shares with me sensations of the moment: did you notice how the choppy waves take on solidity like varnished clay, or see how now it is vitreous, still, one area of incandescence in the distance? One could not be more intimate with nature than is he who made or modified his house precisely for this process of observing, recording every change.

But Father, I protest, here you live inside cerebral exercise but give your body none; it is only when walking one can see the drama of sun setting right, moon rising left, for a time suspended in tandem. Have you forgotten what you told me of the Campidoglio, which you taught me can only be appreciated by the peripatetic spectator? You described an oval in a trapezoid seen by one ascending the magnificent sweeping axis, punctuated by a sharp drop into ruins—falling even deeper into history. And right beside that broad ascent, up the infinitely steep steps of Santa Maria Aracoeli—which those of faith were known to take for sins not yet committed—you, my modern father, who have never seen a church as house of worship, I would have you ascend on your knees in a penitence not prophylactic.

But he will hear no part of it, will only sit absorbed in static reflection, occasionally divulging his impressions, no doubt far less pedestrian than mine. I tend to think of art and nature in more conventional relation than my father. At sunset, I see triptychs composed of cloud and land and light; I see the Sistine Chapel mirrored in these strata, their amazing forms. Yet when the snow is falling thick, it is one blankness, one texture—only faith and habit make it lake—and nearly one color, slightly darker in the lower region, like modern paintings my father urged me to appreciate although they seemed to me unfinished, in fact, unbegun. It was beyond our understanding then, we sisters who since our adolescence knew the difference between Corinthian and Doric column, transept and nave, cantilever, pilaster, trabeation. We knew what part architrave of entablature, what part metope or triglyph of frieze. And yet stalactite vault's relationship to squinch, so simple as it is, eluded me; I tended to confound it with geology: the icicles protruding from our roof, rhyming in turn, in my mind with the shimmery projections of light into lake.

In a box of rocks and marble fragments, I found by chance my tiny replica of the Eiffel Tower (I once pleaded for a souvenir as a slight diversion from his pedantry), reminding me of when he stopped our rented car to lecture on the 984-foot wonder, and never have I lost the tactile memory of the pad of his thumb pressing firmly the lace that edged my blouse, against my clavicle—that part of my anatomy which never failed to elicit admiration on the stage—as if to there imprint its pattern. "This is the essence," he said, "clearer here than in the little toy; the drama of something delicate"—the pressure of his thumb nearly robbed me of breath—"as this lace, welded in steel." The doctor's stethoscope, later pressed a little farther down, probing my chest in search of a rhythm—I thought perhaps detecting Father's thumbprints over me, each time a little farther down. "No, we must not make drama," said the doctor, Daddy's friend the pediatrician—whose house he'd built, "mustn't make a scene—she is an actress, isn't she?"—him smiling at my mother—"I find no damage, see, the heart beats as before." "Oh no, don't give me one thing more to bear," my mother said, when I attempted to confide, as if all the weight of civilization had finally stooped her, reduced her, the collective grandeur of those monuments, remnants, and fragments: Stonehenge, the Pyramids, the Berlin Wall; the Temple at Delphi, the Taj Mahal; the Fountain of Trevi, the Colosseum, and Bernini's angels, I fear, instead of bearing her aloft in ethereal grandeur, were like weights around her wrists and ankles, dragging her silently into the Tevere, so much stone. At Stonehenge, his reverence for those pillars to the sky was as if they were a part of him, then at the Gardens of Kyoto, inside the structure that housed the toilet, as I washed my hands, he pointed out the tiny visual access to a waterfall, held me up to see it; "you see," he said, "how subtly this culture rhymes nature with its architecture."

And now in the cellar, where leaks abound, and leeching lime makes one consistent chalky line that halves the basement wall, and hydrostatic pressure mounts to crack the foundation, he is convinced that scum at the sites of seepage makes for poetry, mimetic correspondence of the grandest order. I plead, Father, shall we snake the sewer, call the plumber? The only garden growing here is mold. I try transcribing faithfully, a secretary of decay, since he will not descend from his observation post (a Monet with his lily-lake, but lacking canvas—my sisters, how we begged to go, to see the pretty pond and bridge; no tourist traps, he scolded us, I try to give you culture, substance: the Temple at Quetzalcoatal, Mosque at Kairawan, Chartre, the Louvre, and Notre Dame). But Father, you might as well have built your own Tarquinian tomb, I feel I'm living in the catacombs, and one day the relics I admire will be my own, our bones, St Anthony's blackened crystal tongue like some otherworldly confection under glass.

What have you learned? What do you in fact infer from the Sicilian temples whose vast columns tower over the sea? Even those which tower no longer delineate in their collapse the sequence of their structuring, offering a map of how they fell;

but those who read it literally, might, as one in attempting to map out the causality of catastrophe, be deluded by illusory retrospective linearity, by logos resurrected out of chaos; so too in our house—everything found through a system of chaos, whether it be gas lamp or dustpan, plunger or wineglass, teapot or road map, ruler, protractor, the stamp book, the White Out, the slide projector's missing bulb, the photo of my mother, already lined, frail, weary, as she waited in a rented car, on a bench, at a newsstand, by a fountain, in a café—Mother, there was a time when the dry ice—when the stalactite squinched my honeycomb—deep inside a vault, the vision of city lights projecting down into water in winter at sunset—burned me in a not-ready place; her "Oh no," like a muffled scream of horror, as from a mouth inside the squeezing skin of a stocking: I see an image on a screen, without sound, of a thousand surfaces shattering, such as one might imagine in some advertisement for a soft drink or ice cream or perfume, a whimpering horror far from emphatic or impassioned, from a woman far too weary to articulate rage or revulsion.

Even now I recall our father's reverence for the ethereal shaft that thrust through the perfect circular aperture of the roof of the perfect circular structure that paid homage to all the gods and which in turn is paid homage to by all the men of his profession. Octopus, I mispronounced that mesmerizing orifice, exchanging consonants, because it trapped him with its tentacles of light. And when I was young, on the form at school—one of the many foreign schools—that asked for my religion, I wrote the cult of Zoroaster and on the next the cult of Zeus. Tell Daddy's

MARY CAPONEGRO

friends what you wrote down—isn't she precious? Do you provide a sacrifice? they joked, and this amused him, perhaps preoccupied him during his pilgrimage to the Pantheon to stand under its coffered dome and trace the sun's diurnal circuit along its tiled floor, as now he gazes on the daily transformations of this liquid body TV screen that never stops transmitting information: lake.

The house in any case may be a testament to his humility, audacity, senility, incompetence; such distinctions more elusive than those between, for instance, metope and triglyph, pylon, proscenium; more esoteric than the concept of entasis; or for that matter, the concept of originality? Everything's falling apart in our house, but then my father always had a strong romantic streak, a thing for ruins. I wonder, are the men of his profession, those who derive an identity from what they erect, more obsessed with vitiation than creation, do they find greater animation in what once was than what is?

Peculiar as this house is, it is less so than his behavior in it, although mine, I need admit, is not exempt: I used floor wax on my point shoes, and stored them inside the freezer; I wore two leotards instead of one, two taut fabric skins across my chest to hold it in, the second's crotch where torso's bulge should be, I mean should have been; for these were secrets of ballerinas, who aspired, as they were trained, to be straight lines upon a stage.

What creates his body's unique suction, I could not surmise. How might one phrase this question to the Sphinx, to whom, of course, my father introduced me at a tender age? "What walks on no legs—on only stomach—evening, morning, noon?" Oh

Sphinx, what do you make of talents such as this, perhaps not far removed from climbing trees? An adaptation, a distortion, of the brazen carefree rituals of youth, as we, in hubris or humility, attempt to enter nature? Even I, who as I mentioned spent long hours at the bar throughout my youth, and could with little toil sustain a vertical relationship between my foot and floor, find this arresting image quite unnerving. Perhaps because my training was so formal, or archaic, this eccentric merge disturbs me; for only when we sleep should we be in such posture, intimate the length of us with surface, while images assault or offer solace—a given, when we close our eyes to dream, we enter what we cannot order—until we resume consciousness, and stand again, unfettered, erect, only the soles of our feet horizontal.

It must be that there are habits we all have that make our neighbors, strangers, intimate ones squeamish, anxious, irritated: how we chew our food, the way we scatter our belongings, perhaps even the timbre of our voice: things we have potential to control, and things beyond control—and I am sure there must have been many things my father found irritating in his children, as they grew and groped and changed, but did not admonish: my shoes in the freezer, glazed in rosin or floor wax, conspicuously absent from the floor; my rehearsals left no time for housework then—as I flitted and fretted and twirled—my shoes freshly frozen, my crotch at my chest; my cunt, I mean heart, on your sleeve. For this he can't be faulted, and I try to bear it this way, with an attitude toward the innocuous idiosyncrasy of someone we hold in high regard; but still I nearly gasp each time I finally

MARY CAPONEGRO

find the ground floor only to find him in the place I don't expect, a place which strikes me as unnatural, at very least inconsistent with convention. True, my salmon-colored point shoes in the freezer never prompted him to raise his voice, but just as certain people stand too close to those with whom they speak, transgressing tacit boundaries of private space, this intimacy transgresses some more subtle spatial code than Father at his drafting table could likely reconcile.

Nor I, not with gesture, word, nor measure, neither increment nor alphabet; as when that man or woman speaking oppresses by proximity, what use to the oppressed her preconceptions or statistics or vocabulary to express the violation of an etiquette that intuition, at least breeding, should make automatic; second nature? The replacement of one law for another? Cicero's alteram naturam is not exactly what I mean, but bridges, roads, and by extension, buildings, are the marks man thrusts into the unsuspecting wilderness. This is craft: intrusion masked as intuition, this is clever alteration such that man can make himself creator in the guise of God to lay these marks upon the earth, thus persuading a perceiver they belong there. But what, I must of somebody inquire, of all the erudite august figures who consorted with my father in my youth, would constitute First Nature? Now that I have seen all the vestiges of the world's great civilizations, you would imagine, through my not entirely voluntary tutelage in mass and void, I'd be amassing wisdom. But such a thing is difficult to gauge; particularly in this circumstance, particularly from discourse with my father, who now desires to be so intimate with nature that no static can interfere, not even the impressions of another, of his daughter. "The dark birds lie like turds, beautiful and perfect, on the surface of the water." I presume he will applaud the singularity of my simile, the tension of its assonance and imagery, but he is not amused, and not impressed; he asks me, "must you vitiate this beauty with distortion?"

I do not reply, because the question is of course rhetorical, and because I do not wish to interrupt my father's contemplation of the body that is sometimes violent, sometimes placid, always liquid light, and I would like to find a way I could be genuinely useful, and perhaps it is only for these reasons that the house has taken on for me a quality of inaccessibility, of awkwardness, as strong a word as threat may be the truest—perceptions which may be akin or wholly different from my father's; I could not pretend to know. But I do know this: in the hollowed-out mystical mountain my father calls his ziggurat, in the solitude of the house's highest, narrowest space, I find myself, though trained in grace, made clumsy as I trip over boxes, and all manner of memorabilia, less the sentimental than professional sort, volumes of *Architectural Digest,* papers and files: everything in the sequence of its now inaudible falling. It's more than just a crawl space—in fact overwhelmingly ample, yet one feels reduced in a sense to all fours. Even I, who could stand on one leg, night or morn or noon, and sometimes none, could never entertain the notion of performing here, for even an audience of one, sissonné or grand jeté, pirouette or echappé. No, never here, where one is always ducking from imagined swooping, slouching just to keep

MARY CAPONEGRO

from bumping my head where the night's creatures might enter and loiter, hanging dormant, ominous, upside down only to burst forth in August from no perceivable cocoon except their solitude. I find their droppings but can't find them—the mess they make is evidence of being yet eludes us: the marks that speak their presence. During colder months, every creak means immanence. I am reminded of our pilgrimage to Lascaux: caves now closed off to the public, Father explained them as churches for animal spirits. Aren't we fortunate, he insisted, to have seen them then?—before they were restricted lest our uncensored breath and sweat and gases accelerate deterioration.

But the only marks on these attic walls are those of decay, age, time, neglect—a place not for activity but storage: screen windows, storm doors, all the wrong size, irrelevant; crutches—likewise too low or too high, from my history of shinsplints and bone spurs and sprains—perhaps it would make as much sense to hobble with those rubber-tipped wooden sticks across a stage, as to stiffen like a statue in some artificial posture while grasped at waist and thigh by a man with a fanciful lump in his stocking (dainty, tumescent, absurd, grotesque)—pictures of my mother, tired, long-suffering (it feels as if my very looking ages her image further), wedding photos, wedding gown (she saved for me; she hoped for all, for any of my sisters, but I was more interested in the coveted forty-pound skirt worn in the Nutcracker—all the ballerinas yearned for its burden; to let that satin broom sweep them across the stage; baby pictures, records of our travels, documentation of my performances, miscellaneous certificates of merit. Et cetera.

In the basement, it is even colder despite the monstrous intermittent noise of the furnace, itself a kind of animal, and the poles are by no stretch of the imagination regal pillars, fluted columns—how delighted was my father once, to visit churches whose hidden spaces served as subterranean showcases for every different kind of column: nothing against which one would be inspired to lean, of course, or stretch one's thigh, facilitating pirouette, entratachat, sissonné, or echappé. Unlike in the attic, there is barely light. On the other hand, it's no mithraeum, and yet it manifests that same paradox—imagine worshiping the god of sun in a space in which its absence is enshrined (a poem I wrote my father when he showed us one: I said, *Pray to sun when there is none.* They laughed about it, the architect friends). I have no poem to offer this house but my thoughts, my homage to its curious vermiculate aspect, which while I don't mean to disparage, I must insist, is not like nature, after all, which one automatically excuses for its deviations (as the tags on garments excuse its fabric, assuring buyer this, which might appear a defect, is in fact organic, and should thus inspire pride instead of shame).

The water's still-more mysterious patterns may appear from afar or viewed briefly, a single rhythm, all motion or all stillness, but my own study (and who knows, perhaps my father's too) reveals an intricate sequence of incremental variation, so subtly out of sync that they are in effect a unity, like a school of fish or flock of geese as we sometimes see inhabiting this site, or something on a more primitive organic level: a wriggling mass such as

MARY CAPONEGRO

one might see under a microscope, a collective body moving forward as one music.

My father wants to be flush with the lake—he wants to be literally at sea level, as in the Turkish houses he insisted we experience from inside; he wants to view seated or supine, reclining, through low window lines, without surrendering nature.

But I am afraid that one day I shall ascend from the cave of the labyrinthine basement or descend from the attic maze to view him through the vast picture window-wall, as well as through the liquid glass of lake itself, allowing me to see his frail body sinking deeper into vitreous abyss. The contours of his features, lost in the lake's own lineaments, will at first be discernible like the boundaries between the rocks perpetually submerged there, then recede, his identity sinking under my vision, my grasp: inaccessible, irretrievable; and in no way then could I for all my training in extension and contortion of limbs resuscitate or rescue him, and his floating form will haunt my dreams: his sleeping, fetal form. And how then will I reconcile my ambiguous matrix of images? And how will I bear the sight of monuments, cathedrals, even supermarkets, beauty parlors; for what thing, tell me, sphinx, tell me, oracle, tell me, shaman, what thing on earth is devoid of structure? How shall I bear to maintain this curious house, which of course it will be my legacy to inherit? I will dance as if in ritual atonement or bereavement—I who must atone for others' sins, I whose grief precedes this one—I'll dance before the setting sun to keep the illusion of equilibrium as I nightly drown.

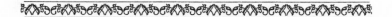

THE MOTHER'S MIRROR

It is commonly known that those nearest to us, those of whom we have the most extensive, intimate knowledge, are often held at arm's length in our minds. The saying rolls so easily off the tongue: "familiarity breeds contempt," and the idiom "to take for granted" is as familiar to us as those we do. An elaborate system inevitably—yet inadvertently—evolves whereby we offer such permissions to each other.

Thus even as we hold our spouse's hand, or feel with genuine concern the tepid forehead of our firstborn, we simultaneously regard the ridge of black under the former's nails, the tiny white specks that fall to his shoulders when we smooth back his hair, and when our eyes travel furtively down, they settle on the latter's scuffed, untied shoes, his toe beginning to emerge from the leather like an egg in the very process of hatching.

The foot inside that shoe is not often idle as we speak to the flesh of our flesh, our firstborn son, as we speak with the intention of exchanging pleasantries, conveying affection; to elicit tenderness, or heaven forbid, solicit information. The foot taps; it jabs the ground. Our reluctant interlocutor's replies are listless; his eyes elsewhere, anywhere but in contact with our own.

Perhaps we keep our disappointment to ourself or perhaps we voice it, and once articulated, it is all too seductive to make a ritual of the words, as if they were beads of a rosary and we gathered by each repetition indulgences instead of alienation. As luck would have it, any replies which we receive do no more than inform of complications, superstitions, idiosyncrasies, compulsions: in short, excuses. The shoes, for example, have grown to have sentimental value; it is too unmanly to fuss with one's cuticles; least rational of all is our husband's insistence that excessive washing of the hair may cause it in time to thin, to recede, and eventually, to fall out. Is that what we want?

What would be the point, in the wake of such a confrontation, in trying to address our younger daughter's ostentatious makeup and jewelry, the revealing bodice of her dress—on those occasions when she does dress—or more usually, as today, the threadbare sites on her dungarees? From the time of her conception, we had imagined a special closeness with our daughter: the seeking of advice, the poignant offering of secrets, both joyful and anxious, the sharing of that which is distinctly feminine—at least, as we construe the word. And yet the girl is more sullen even than her brother, less forthcoming in our presence, mistrustful for no reason we can possibly surmise. And if we are so bold as to critique the company she keeps, allude to standards of behavior, or imply that certain activities might be less than edifying, her terse reply will put us in our place: what can an old-fashioned housewife know of contemporary mores, styles; advances in our culture? This is not our business, nor our metier.

Thus, after actual or imagined encounters, all the more frustrated, we find ourself admiring obsessively the graceful countenance, the courteous demeanor of our colleagues or our supervisor—granted we refer to the part-time employment of a woman who is principally a housewife, whose image is a fixed one, in community, in family—but regardless of the context, we cannot turn away our gaze from the prominent cheekbones or delicate wrists of strangers, or cease to dwell upon the uncanny way some women's stockings never sag below the knee—as ours inevitably do after only an hour of wear—or how some stylish men manage never to display an inch of flesh between top of sock and hem of pant. Why is that strip of flesh so bothersome to us—appearing to glow in the dark as he sits in the living room chair in our home? Why do we find ourself enraptured by the sonorous voice or elegant meaningless gestures of those we do not harbor in our homes? We are given to imagining, increasingly, how fulfilling life might be if it were he or she or they whom we greeted at table every morning, dined with every evening, perhaps by candlelight, without the television's ubiquitous, intrusive presence; perhaps even held, in certain circumstances—when we allow ourself the thought—in our embrace; the weary sequences of habit replaced by spontaneous rather than contractual affection, replaced by—might it ever be?—incendiary fervor?

Just take a look at yourselves, we want to cry; just for once would you listen to yourselves, to the persons of our household who seemed at one time to take more pride in their appearance, to be more refined in their behavior, more courteous, more appreciative of ourself? For recently it seems that when an individual is needed for any task, be it rising wearily to make his coffee, or driving to the pharmacy for yet another urgent errand, or cleaning out debris in the garage, it is the hand attached to our already strained shoulder which rises automatically to volunteer.

Yet should not one who regularly offers services, who does one's share, be given also certain compensations? Should not such persons be allowed to make, occasionally, demands? There must be some control over the degree to which we take each other for granted. How, for instance, have we spent this evening? With hardly a thought to our comfort. It may be that what others think of as necessity has been transformed in our perception into luxury; so that, for instance, we consider it less troublesome to ignore the fullness of our bladder than to interrupt her cosmetic application—an at-least-once daily ritual requiring intense concentration—or than to knock so loudly as to be heard over the sound produced by our firstborn when in his throat he does the internal acrobatics of suspending flavored liquid with the intention of freshening his breath before a visit from his girlfriend. The sound is in fact so comical to our ears, reminding us as it does of the gurgling of his early years, that it increases our urgency even as we strive to ignore the insistent pressure; we

34 ~~⌐

must cover our mouth with our hand lest we laugh out loud, or worse. And we may have to hold out longer still, for it is likely that he has negotiated with his sister over who precedes the other in the bathroom, and she will need to linger long before the mirror, taking to her eyes what would appear to be an instrument of torture, and with the clamped end, forcing the defenseless lashes into sculpted curl.

Not only are our physiological functions hindered by these rituals; pragmatic matters of the house are left on hold as well. We would like to start the laundry, so his sweatshirt and her ragged dungarees will be available on demand. We would like to let the dishwasher initiate its cycle, now that we have cleared away all traces of the repast we spent the afternoon preparing. Ingeniously we have fit all the vessels into the wire racks of the appliance: the pots and pans and flatware, even the tiny plate on which we put our own supper—the full-sized dinner plate that completes the Blue Danube pattern china set was accidentally broken recently—his girlfriend is our guess, but we are not so small, so petty, as to mention it, make issue of it—and we would not want to ask any other family member to make the sacrifice of crowding food onto such a diminutive surface. Still we are tentative about pressing the oval silver button that starts the cycle, lest we alter the consistency of our husband's bath— known to last over an hour—or perhaps the children's showers are now in progress: those pre-trysting rituals during which the steam rises and disseminates to fog not only the bathroom mirror, but all the windows of the house, as if our family resided in the humidity of the tropics rather than the temperate climate of a Northeastern suburb of the United States.

How much is it to ask that we use the facilities; who but ourself would hesitate? Certainly not our firstborn, who, when a toddler, never did so before barging in on our privacy. (This too, so long ago, may have contributed to the shaky condition of our bladder.) We should not ask at all; we should announce, by fiat, our intention. The door is unlikely to be locked. No one would be aghast, for there is not a prima donna in the house: such are the permissions of domestic familiarity. Nor are we or any member of the family inclined to give excessive priority to propriety in this house, where the men are likely to come to dinner in their undershorts, and our daughter to wear as street clothes what most women would deem inappropriate for private lounging.

Why is it then, that when we form a fist before the door we cannot bring ourself to make contact in such crude fashion? It seems intrusive, so that at the last moment we resort to stealth; for if the door is unlocked, then knocking is not a functional prerequisite to entry, and we need not disturb whomever now occupies the bathroom; we only need perform one humble function, after all. If a shower is in progress—as the sounds we hear would now indicate—the curtain might preserve discretion. (We have heard that in fancy European hotels, bath and bidet are altogether separate spheres of activity.) Yes, clearly an outburst is unnecessary; obtaining the far more modest objective should be our focus—so intent a focus, in fact, by this point, that we cannot waste a moment in knocking, or for that matter looking at

MARY CAPONEGRO

what lies before us as we make our way, purposefully, through the steam, to lower the toilet seat—always raised, it seems—to sit in mingled pain and relief of micturition—damn, blood again (we did not mean to swear out loud)—this is the consequence of trying to train one's bladder; our organs are not circus animals, after all; we should not wait so long; we are ridiculous; our dubious heroism is destructive; will we ever learn?

In our vexation, and then resignation, we raise our eyes to see, in the corner, our husband, his back to us. He makes rapid movements with his hand, his elbow pumping up and down: gestures which, when he turns his head to see who has sworn, turn furtive; but when he continues, too intent on his objective to cease, he cannot stifle his expression of catharsis: an ecstatic sound we can barely recall from his mouth as his own momentarily vertical stream finds more joyful release.

We applaud; we blow him a kiss, surprising him. (Never were we one to resent the good fortune of others, no matter the contrast with our own circumstance.) He is unsure of how to react; he had not expected an audience, particularly not our approval, is suspicious of it, we would guess. And then we see, through the admittedly obnubilating mist, that all of them are present: in our company, in the bathroom—though removed, at the same time, preoccupied. Their distance, however, has a different quality than usual. Through the semitransparent curtain we see the most curious silhouettes: flawless, agile bodies, as if in choreographed ensemble, seen through scrim: dramatic, seductive, mesmerizing. The vision seems to have one hundred arms,

like the Indian goddess, so swift and graceful are their movements. How much we wish to peel away the membrane separat-
ing beauty from beholder.

And is there obstacle? No greater than there was to opening the door. Although our mission is, as it were, accomplished,
we are transfixed; we cannot make ourself depart. Gently, stealthily, we draw back the curtain. They will not be distracted by its
whisper, so engaged are they in their activities, which, when
unsheathed, seem both ordinary and exalted. Has the mist begun
to dissipate, or have our eyes begun to adjust? It would seem
some seal was broken when we first opened the door.

Uninterrupted, and un-self-conscious in their nakedness,
the group of them are painting on the tiles, in flamboyant brush-
strokes, what appears to be a mural; the scene seems tropical,
lush, idyllic. It seems, in fact, to expand before our eyes. A small
child we have never seen before completes the party, molding a
tower of the waterlogged remains of the transparent bar in the
soap dish: quite an impressive edifice; his eyes wide before his
own accomplishment. Our daughter's leg, meanwhile, is raised as
if in pirouette, as he, the one for whom she spent the evening
"dressing," glides a manual razor tenderly, deftly, up her calf, making, eventually, a circle around her leg, while she attempts to do
the same procedure to his face and upper lip. Given the awkwardness of synchronizing his head down, her hand above, they
take, eventually, to lying down, reclining the length of their bodies in the bath, despite the waterfall that rains down upon them
all the while, in order to make the mutual gesture. Then, when

MARY CAPONEGRO

the flesh of face and calf are silken-smooth, each, facing the other, dangles one foot out of the tub, while taking clippers to each toenail in sequence. There is not a nick for all the contact with sharp instruments, not a drop of blood.

The unfamiliar child has completed his slippery castle and embraces it to slide down, finding the slender clippings piled on the side of the tub; he marvels at them as if they were luminous seashells at the beach; perhaps he contemplates including them in his composition as a decorative addition. Instead, he blows into a plastic flute, making surprisingly articulate tones. Is that our eldest son behind him, building a boat, with more alacrity than we have ever witnessed him exhibit? And more skill. In less than a minute, it seems, he has crafted the bow, the stern, the ship entire; then down the drain he sails, a disappearing act; even the others are momentarily distracted from their independent activities to gape, as when a woman is sawed in half by a magician. No sooner has he submerged than he resurfaces, only to repeat the cycle over and over, the others applauding at each completion of his round trip.

Our husband, meanwhile, who initially drew our eye, having completed his goal, is celebrating with acrobatic maneuvers of even greater magnitude: swinging from the curtain rod—hopefully sturdy enough—with the dexterity of a professional; movements of which we never knew him capable. After he has warmed up with a series of chin-ups—the bar, too, seems to have a resilience beyond the ordinary—he does more intricate balletic maneuvers, employing his hands as if they were feet; his feet as if hands. We cannot, again, restrain ourself from applauding, and he seems less self-conscious, less ambivalent, in this mode than before.

But lest we embarrass or intimidate or compromise him with our gaze, we let our eyes wander to the other members of the troupe. Our daughter's boyfriend is now vigorously lathering her hair. How attractive she is without makeup. If only the world could glimpse her freshness: to see the sweet serenity behind the harsher mask. By the same token, our son, for the first time since adolescence, appears not to be slouching.

We have fallen into paradise through the most mundane of circumstances. How lovely to think of the effortless transformations! We cannot wait to view our own, which surely, by osmosis, must occur. With a facecloth from the linen closet we wipe the mirror of steam, quickly, before it has a chance to form again. We will smile at the image of ourself, with lips like those we see on these exalted faces, lips resembling ripest summer fruit. How wondrous is the world and its discoveries!

But the mouth that looks back at us from the defogged reflective surface is, on the contrary, brittle, and the nostrils above, thin and severe. We whimper to see the wrinkles, even more numerous than we had imagined, the deeply furrowed brow, and the puffiness of the lids that can only partially mask the icy candor of our once quite striking blue eyes.

MARY CAPONEGRO

THE FATHER'S
BLESSING

Allow me, if you would, to tell you of a wedding, which took place not long ago, a wedding no different from any other—not objectively—in which I played my role to everyone's satisfaction, at least initially. For all I know, the bride might have been already with child when I performed the rite, but I would never be so crude as to count months upon my fingers, when I hear of joyous news, for these very fingers may be called upon to cradle the wailing infant's tender head at christening time, to give him support as he enters new terrain, unaware of the security, solace, and spiritual wealth that define it. To him, at that moment, I must seem merely a stranger offering unfamiliar, disturbing sensations. But later in his life he will realize the value of my gesture, and our bond.

The parents of this hypothetical child are perhaps another matter: the couple I recently wed, for instance; they were, in my opinion, naive. They did not realize the contract they were making—with me, that is—when they asked if I would sanctify their union. They assumed they could bid me good riddance, I expect, once the vows were exchanged, as if the rite were mere formality.

How strangely they regarded me when—after I had played my role to the satisfaction of all, from the solemnity of the vows to the levity of the reception, chatting pleasantly, even wittily, with the parents, both sets, commenting in passing on the beauty of the bride, lest they think me at too great a remove from human experience—when there was a lull in the receiving line, I took the couple aside (who would question my doing it?) and asked if they would have me perform the last rites.

Without affectation or cynicism, I announced, "I live, as you know, in the rectory far away, and there is always the chance—though etiquette prohibits our acknowledging—that should you summon me at the last minute, I would be unable to reach you in time. There are so few of us, exiguously placed, and the parishes likewise scarce. The road to the rectory is seldom plowed in winter, and in spring the potholes impede smooth travel. When it rains, the roads turn almost instantly to clay, so that only in a skillful driver's hands and at high speeds can they be traversed successfully. If I were to administer the sacrament to one of you now, think of the time and anxiety we all might be spared, and the law of averages indicates that the partner to receive this prophylactic blessing would likely be the party to require it later on. I realize it is hard to think ahead in the bloom of youth. . . ."

The bride, aghast, clutched the arm of the man who only hours ago had been made, under my aegis, her husband, and challenged him by her fear to confront me, which he, I must admit, quite eloquently did; no doubt a heroic effort to match

　　　　　　　　　　　　　　　　　　　MARY CAPONEGRO

my own eloquence and to impress her by trying to rhyme with my authority. "Father," he scolded, "what can be your intent? This is a time of rejoicing. You yourself pronounced the words, 'till death do us part.' Would you part us so soon then?"

Realizing that I had been misunderstood, I, who am an accommodating man—I do not proselytize, do not force myself—desisted (my objectives were unlikely to be understood within that public context—for heads were beginning to turn; those who had passed through the line were beginning to gravitate toward it again) and promptly took my leave, against the parents' puzzled protests: "Do visit us again soon, Father." And I had the sense, even as I gracefully accepted defeat, that I would see them all again soon enough.

Walking in town to collect myself, I realized there was another related visit I could make, to clarify what had been muddled. And so I sought out an acquaintance, or might one say, a colleague: the owner, as it happens, of a funeral home. Indeed, the bride and groom appeared surprised when I returned, accompanied, much later in the evening, to the family's house, where the wedding had taken place—the reception had been elsewhere, as is the custom. Little could they appreciate my willingness, my eagerness, to initiate them into a yet deeper mystery than the one upon which they had already, by laws of convention, embarked, allegedly for the first time. I even brought my friend the undertaker with me—he required considerable persuasion—to reinforce what might otherwise seem mere words, and to balance the awkwardness of a third party lest they misinterpret my intentions.

The undertaker and I allowed no ambiguity in our presentation; we were straightforward, precise.

"I've come," he said, just as I instructed him, barely glancing at the two individuals he addressed, "to take the measurements for the casket. Would you be so kind as to lie apart, upon your backs, hands folded so, and I'll be through in no time." They seemed in shock, paralyzed, in their melded state, until the undertaker brought forward his implement to measure the bridegroom's member.

"All parts are parts of the whole," was his speech; "all shall come to dust." Meanwhile the groom hid himself the more deeply inside his bride, as if this would render the whole of him invisible. The bride's cry I could not pretend to interpret; perhaps she was pleased to offer him haven, or startled by his urgency; yet I would have thought the volume appropriate to an instance of assault. The ruler may as well have been a dagger: such was her alarm. Or did she fear that to which she had been newly joined would be, by the former's measure, reduced. Who can possibly surmise the unbridled musings of the young in unfamiliar circumstances in a world relentlessly novel? I suppose in some ways the equanimity of a man of the cloth is an enviable thing.

Because I am a sincere man I must tell you that there is indeed advantage to the closet called confessional: one can be so close, intimate; only a thin screen separates oneself from the sinner, one's own sagacious voice from the whispers which reveal the deepest secrets. That is our special privilege; one might say power: that no one can justify surprise or suspicion when I appear on the other side of, by extension, any partition. There is, with me, potentially greater intimacy than that between a man and wife: one bound to breed resentment, foster ambivalence; for people are uncomfortable robbed of accusations: meddler, eavesdropper, peeping tom, spy; no one of these terms applies to a man of my vocation.

Father is the name by which all know me, the term by which I'm ceaselessly addressed. But was that the sound that echoed in mythic Daedalus's ears long after he'd watched the flesh of his flesh falling inexorably from air into water: Father? Father? I am the man who must give answers; thus expectation begets my ingenuity, for I want them prepared, as one does one's children. And I, like any parent, will never learn my sermon's lesson: that they must have their own experience; one cannot spare them. The more you try the more they will reject, be repelled—and thereby eject themselves from the sky. Seldom are they equipped to receive the truth, though one wants to believe sheer force of one's sincerity will smooth the roughest road, quarry hardest stone. Yet one must exercise caution, for sincerity is a dangerous thing.

It was caution that dictated I depart, with my accomplice, allowing the other two to sort through their admittedly challenging instruction. A man in my profession must be bold, as He whom I revere was bold, but never reckless. The long journey back to the rectory is always an ideal opportunity for reflection.

As I might have guessed, no sooner had the season changed—or so it seemed; perhaps it had changed more than once—than I received a summons: I was needed. It must, I thought, be time for the baptism now. As my sense of direction is acute, my memory guided me accurately to the town, the tree-lined avenue, the stately Victorian house which was the Callahan residence and inside it, the very chamber from which I had once been banished. I was unable to persuade the undertaker to accompany me this time; from his point of view the prior experience had bred only humiliation. His profession has not taught him, as mine has, the value, the necessity, of perseverance. I would represent him, as I represented so many already. I had my vial of holy water and prayer book in hand as I entered the house of the bride's parents, the same in which the ceremony had occurred. I assumed I would lead the family to the church after exchanging pleasantries, becoming reacquainted. Perhaps I would hold the child once we arrived, so that my hand upon him would not feel strange when the ritual was enacted.

But when I arrived, the cries I heard were not an infant's, but those of a mature woman, and that is how I came to grace the threshold of their chamber, for I ascended the staircase to investigate with the intention of assisting. As I squinted through the crack in the door, I saw the mother to be perspiring, panting, writhing, from time to time moaning in effort of that singular process of which I can perforce have no inkling, called *labor,* derived from Eve's seduction by a serpent. Even a husband, it is said, cannot soothe a woman during this arduous period; but I who as a priest possess potentially greater intimacy, thought to humbly offer solace.

"I am here," I said, through the crack which gave me witness.

"No," she screamed, I assumed to the source of her pain.

And when she repeated it over and over, I questioned whether contractions could be so frequent. I realized I possessed not even clinical knowledge regarding this miraculous yet commonplace event. I felt something akin to shame, before her next and more explicit statement jarred me from the sentiment: "It's that horrid priest again!" Her husband rushed to the door and said diplomatically, "There must be some mistake, Father; we sent for the midwife, to assist delivery. It was planned that we have a home birth."

I replied that I found it odd they had chosen this alternative with a hospital down the street.

"Father," the groom was losing his studied patience, "medicine—am I correct?—is not your area of expertise, and our affairs are not your—he used His name in vain—business. Besides, isn't it obvious that my wife is in no condition to travel, even a short distance, at this stage? On the other hand, there is nothing to hold you here. If priests are in as scarce supply as you report, then I would not want it on my conscience that we had monopolized you."

As the groom spoke, admittedly with cleverness, I realized that the suggestion that served his convenience was not without substance, for if it was the case that the couple had not summoned me, then some miscommunication must have occurred through the secretary at the rectory, and some other couple required my ministrations in some fashion. But before I could take action, the most searing cry of all pierced the air, and the woman, to whom the groom turned again to face, and who had previously appeared distorted only in the distention of her abdomen, now manifested a most peculiar symmetry, for she possessed two heads, one at each end. We stood transfixed by this sight, suspended in time, in awe, until the bride herself corrected this anomaly as she pushed out—with disconcertingly audible discomfort, through that chamber that will ever be a secret to me—a diminutive whole human being.

The completed act restored us to our senses and he dismissed me, saying, "Father, you must not distract me any longer. I have neglected my wife at her most critical hour. She must have no disturbance now. If you want to make yourself useful, you might go find the midwife for us." Then with his foot he closed the slender aperture that had been my access to the two, now three.

Although for reasons other than those the groom believed, it was, I felt, my duty to explore elsewhere. The hospital was my destination for there was very likely another couple, another newborn, with whom I had business, a family more receptive to that business. I recalled the pleasant and devout man and woman I had married quite some time ago, who had wanted nothing in the world as much as children, but the pregnancies had been in every case problematic; I knew not the details of the matter.

When I arrived at the hospital, after quietly exiting the house, I walked immediately to the front desk and offered the name of this prior couple. The nurse recognized my attire, and directed me to the room where the wife had recently given birth. The couple received me gratefully, but they were not alone. A doctor was with them, as well as several others I presumed to be medical students, peering at a polaroid photograph. My presence did not distract them from their concentration, nor their discussion, the focal point of which seemed to be the ascription of blame, and which became increasingly agitated. I was, I eventually realized, too late, although I blessed the recently departed child, gone to God no sooner had he exited the womb, strangled by the very cord which bound him to his mother's nurture, in the act of being born. Ah, to witness life and death in such proximity; what more profound instruction could one receive? Although I was too late in one sense, the gift of this lesson was not denied me, and my duty was to offer it to those who could most profit from it. I granted myself permission to borrow documentation.

I hastened from the room to the corridor to the elevator and so on, until I was once again at the Callahan's residence. As I was the last to leave, the door had not been latched, so I let myself in; then, like a child, I took the steps two at a time until I stood before the door of the bride and groom. I knocked before entering and addressed them by their Christian names.

"Kathleen," I cried, "David. There is something I must show you. Something you must see."

"Where's the midwife, Father?" the groom asked with little animation, concentrating on the pulsating cord that sustained mother and child as unity, clamped at two sites with paper clips, above which he held a small blunt scissors, moving them between two different sites only inches apart, unable to decide, it seemed, where to sever the bond, or simply unable to bring himself to make the cut. The thing which eluded him seemed to me some dense but slender fish, perhaps an eel, caught between sea and land, its respiration intact despite its dislocation. Through the power of grace, it had not been an infelicitous agent in this instance.

"Here in my hand," I replied, "in my very hand." I held the picture to the light. "Kathleen," I whispered tenderly to her weary form, her sweat-drenched face. I knelt beside her, conscious of, yet not repelled by the odor of sweat and flesh that pervaded the room, the sight of the bright white linen stained with blood. "This is for you."

She squinted at the image I held before her, then gazed at me incredulously before releasing a sound whose frequency seemed almost too high for human ears. Hurriedly, I veiled the truth again, covering what had been for a moment visible. Moments of the truth are all we can bear. And in the next, the midwife arrived. (I heard the bride's mother answer the bell, explaining that she refused to get involved; her participation had not been invited, and could anyone imagine how difficult it must be to listen to a daughter's cries and feel so impotent?)

The newest guest appeared before us, and promptly took charge. Regarding the bride's glazed eyes and distorted expression (and no doubt informed by the shriek preceding her entry), she said, "What happened here?" The groom motioned toward me, using the scissors as a teacher might a pointer, but spoke no

MARY CAPONEGRO

words. "Father, it would be better if you left me alone with her."
Then she addressed the groom. "I'm sorry I was delayed. A
breech birth at the hospital involved unforseen complications
and I was called in to help." After a pause, she added, "unfortunately to no avail." She gently released the rounded handles of
the implement from his grip, then lay her hand on Kathleen's
forehead, and I was struck by how similar to a sacramental gesture was this contact. "David, you should accompany the
Reverend, since Kathleen will need complete rest to recover
from the trauma. I doubt she'll be able to nurse."

After performing with expediency the maneuver the
groom had been unable to execute, the midwife lifted the tiny
form, wrapped it carefully in a blanket she had brought, and
handed it to me, then quickly corrected herself, offering it to the
groom. Once the bundle was dispensed with, she took the bride's
wrist between her thumb and fingers, feeling for a rhythm I suspect she feared absent. "If only I could have gotten here on
time," she said to herself, no longer communicating with the
groom and myself, shaking her head with concern at the bride's
vacant face. Then she repeated it, like a dirge.

Remembering our presence, she instructed and bid us
depart, promising to send word when things stabilized. Who
were we to doubt her? "It makes most sense for the baby to be
cared for in maternity at the hospital, until Kathleen revives." She
lay the infant in its father's arms, whispering, "such a lovely little
boy." The groom followed me, reluctant but obedient, out the
door, while she set about with her humble instruments, wiping,

sponging, disinfecting. We heard her strained but authoritative voice behind us: "And buy some formula, in the hospital pharmacy, in case we need it later."

My second trip to the hospital, then, was a simple twofold errand. David, as soon as we reached the building, adopted a rapid pace; I assumed that his strategy was to divide our errands for the sake of maximum efficiency. After clearing the front desk with a nod from the receptionist, I rode the elevator to the room where I had first been inspired by the photograph. Having been unprepared for Kathleen's strong reaction to it, I now wondered whether I needed to protect the stillborn's mother from the reminder of what she had seen, as it were, in the flesh; of her flesh. Probably she too should not be disturbed, regardless of how welcoming the two appeared.

Discreetly I slipped the Polaroid under their door, face down, and rode the elevator back to street level to find the pharmacy. It was clearly marked and a woman from behind the counter offered me assistance.

"I have been instructed," I began, but could not manage to complete the sentence; it seemed awkward.

"There is a woman," I began anew.

She raised her eyes. "Yes, Father?"

"A mother."

She lowered them again.

"Her milk . . ."

"I understand perfectly, Father. There is no need to continue."

MARY CAPONEGRO

And she turned her back to me to search the shelves behind her, before handing me a box approximately ten inches high. I felt inside my cassock for my billfold, but she placed her own hand over mine to stop me.

"Please, Father," she said. "We know about the tragedy. The hospital staff is very concerned, and supportive. Some of us feel the word"—she whispered it—"ashamed"—"is not too strong. In any case, do let this be our contribution."

"But, Miss," I protested, fearful of appearing ungrateful or obtuse. "I am not certain I have made myself clear, or if I myself am clear, regarding the equipment that is . . . needed."

"I am a woman, Father," she said, with gravity and unflinching gaze. "I know things you cannot know. Trust me."

I had no response to her authority and conviction. I could only go back to the Callahan's, perhaps not correctly but at least not empty-handed. David may have been required to remain with the child, and it was best for one of us to be available.

This time, however, I did not venture upstairs, but remained in the lower portion of the house, seeking refuge in a room, to the rear of the staircase—a room immaculate and austere, containing a long oak table and eight matching straight-backed chairs with brocade seats, upon one of which I sat. I slid the package to the far end of the polished table, then laid my head in my hands, resting this weight on the smooth wooden surface. After some time I lifted up my head, taking several deep breaths, the last exhalation interrupted by the appearance of Mrs. Callahan, mother of the bride.

"Father Faraday, what a lovely surprise! Have you come to say Mass at St. Agnes?"

"No, Mrs. Callahan," I said, regaining my composure—a man who must attend, through the vehicle of a single sense, to a sequence of stories, of lives, of sins whose range spans from the barely worth mentioning to the most debased; a man who must juxtapose the only confession in the life of an evil person with the routine inflated guilts of an exemplary practitioner; such a man has evolved the skill of flexibility, of quick recovery; to use the colloquial metaphor of our automobile-dependent culture, the ability to switch gears—"No, another appointment,"—there was no need to be specific—"now completed." Talking was easier than I'd anticipated, even reassuring.

"All the better, Father; you can join us then, for our Sunday meal," she said, unfolding an embroidered white cloth and spreading it over the table, letting it billow out as one might a bedsheet. "I'm sure the children will be delighted."

"I wouldn't assume anything, Mrs. Callahan." I thought she had not heard me; she was already through the door, then back again, the first of numerous trips to heap the Lord's bounty onto the table: steaming platters, casseroles, a roast ready to be carved.

"You must excuse the children," she said, as if there had been no interruption to our conversation, and as she continued to lay out the meal, concluding with, as afterthought, a bottle of fine red wine, and another Waterford glass. "They are not beholden to tradition, as our generation was." She smiled at me, pausing in her activity. "They will appear when it suits them."

"Shall I begin carving?" I asked, as she began to light the candles in the candelabra, no trace of concern marring her flawless countenance as the flame drew nearer and nearer her slender fingers. I was fatigued and felt less in command of my expressions. I feared Mrs. Callahan might have thought me greedy rather than eager to offer a gesture of assistance; I was ashamed of how much effort she had expended while I sat immobile in my temporary stupor.

"The one favor I would ask of you, Father Faraday, is to say grace for us, if it wouldn't be too much of an imposition—not until everyone arrives, of course." She sighed, and seemed to raise her voice slightly when she added wistfully, "if we could just for once all be together at the table." She sighed again.

"Mrs. Callahan," I sought to console her, "I would urge you to consider that your daughter and son-in-law may be occupied with matters of some significance, and their absence is not necessarily an expression of indifference or hostility. Or, for that matter, ingratitude."

"No, indeed, Father," she replied, and with dignity continued, "but you, as a man of the cloth, are unlikely to be acquainted with that wrenching feeling, that torture of wanting to intervene, wanting to make available the wisdom of maturity, but knowing you must not surrender to it, for if you do, every strategy will go awry before your eyes."

Mrs. Callahan was visibly moved by what she shared, as was I to be receiving her words—more than she knew—and she permitted herself to digress: "Everything today is natural.

But would the Lord have allowed man the mind to evolve technology if he meant him to be left to only natural devices? You are obviously the expert here, Father, excuse my . . . trespassing." She half-smiled. "I asked them, what is wrong with a good old-fashioned hospital? Now, I was a nurse, Father Faraday, before the Lord blessed our marriage with a child, and I know a bit about these matters, but we left to doctors the work of doctors and did not monkey around, if you'll excuse the expression, with life and death. There are risks, are there not, in every natural process?"

"You are a thoughtful woman, Mrs. Callahan."

"I suppose you might as well begin the carving," she said, resigned; "otherwise we may be waiting here until everything is cold." As I could infer the tenderness of the meat from its succulent aroma, I was more than willing to comply. "It is nice to have a man about, to lend a hand. My husband, you see, he's been . . . unwell."

"I'm very sorry to hear that." My memory of Mr. Callahan at the wedding—robust, energetic—was difficult to reconcile with these words—unless I confused him with the father of the groom; I did not think this was the case. And yet, our world fluctuates before us daily; appearances ever-unreliable indices of truth.

"The Lord works in mysterious ways; isn't that right, Father Faraday?"—as if she'd read my mind. I could not decipher her tone: conspiratorial, mocking, perhaps even . . . flirtatious? Fortunately, the moment of intense ambiguity passed.

"So much in life is confusing, isn't it? Nothing more so

than being a parent in this day and age—I'm sure you've heard the stories, Father. In fact, I wonder if I might be so bold as to impose upon you for an even larger favor—since we may not get to grace, at this rate." She made an enigmatic gesture with her mouth, that seemed half sinister, half coquettish, or perhaps neither, some neutral expression colored by my fatigue? My job—I thank the Lord—is not to judge, outside a certain circumscribed, sacred enclosure. "My daughter, I'm convinced, is in need of guidance," she said, "guidance beyond my capacity. I thought marriage would make a difference, but I'm afraid that in some ways, it's only made things worse, and I wondered—I thought, perhaps, if you went up, and spoke with her . . ."

"I would like to very much, Mrs. Callahan," I said sincerely, "very much indeed; but there are times when no one, not even a man of God, can take the place of a mother." As I said the last word I rose to procure the package that had remained undisturbed (but for Mrs. Callahan's occasional furtive glances)—then returned to the seat, placing on the table its contents: a box which I began to push toward her slowly.

"What can it be?" she asked, staring at the thing as if it would speak its name.

I continued to push with my fingers the device I had purchased at the hospital pharmacy. Both of us regarded its incremental progress as a child might a caterpillar's. It whispered across the tablecloth: my fingers its gentle engine. When the box had achieved sufficient distance to be within close range, I drew back my hand and remained silent while she studied the labeling. Mrs.

Callahan blushed, giggled, and then rose, smoothing the front of her blouse, and I was reminded, for some reason, of the expression *blushing bride.*

"You are admirably down to earth, Father Faraday, and yet so . . . discreet. Please do help yourself while I have a brief chat with my daughter." She grasped the box, tentatively at first, but then walked decisively out of the room, to the stairs. Would Kathleen be conscious? Would her mother's presence rouse her if not, and stimulate her healing? I hoped it would be so, but my own hunger distracted me from this concern.

In truth, I could not remember the last time I had eaten. Had I even had breakfast? I carved a few slices of beef—it should certainly not go to waste, this bounty—and there was no point in serving Mrs. Callahan's portion only to watch it grow cold. I passed myself the green beans, the roast potatoes. With the first bite, I realized I was ravenous. What a relief it was to nourish myself without the burden of conversation, to leave the world, for just a few moments, to its own devices.

I ate much more rapidly than was salubrious. Perhaps this was the source of my indigestion, although I suspect it had more to do with the bride's raised voice, followed by the shattering of glass. I laid down my fork, went back to the living room, and leaned against the banister once again, wincing at the words toward which I could not keep myself from straining.

"You're positively medieval, Mother." At least the bride possessed the energy to raise her voice. The midwife had either cured her—one of the innumerable daily miracles we take for

MARY CAPONEGRO

granted—or misapprehended the situation from the start. Perhaps the former was now with David and the child, and all would return shortly.

"Darling, that is very discourteous. The breast pump was a gift from Father Faraday."

"The priest! Mother, you must be kidding. That man is very peculiar."

"He's not a man exactly, is he—a priest? But I think he's quite nice, dear, and you were rude to him."

"No, mother, he was . . . cruel to me; you can't imagine."

"I'm sure you exaggerate, Kathleen; he performed the ceremony so beautifully. He keeps in touch, and you can tell he cares. I sense he's very . . . trustworthy."

I slowly climbed the stairs, no more rapidly than I had pushed the problematic box, now discarded. I climbed almost against my will. Certain projects seem to have no end in sight, before we gain the profit of perspective. Yet we must never cease to strive, to hope. It seemed that the voices grew muted as I drew near.

"Mother, I feel nervous when I know he's around, and I'm feeling weak as it is. We need a quiet place to talk. There's just too much going on here, and he is a man after all, no matter what any of you say."

"Well of course, dear, technically, that's true. But a priest is a special kind of man, and if you can't trust a priest, whom can you trust? It isn't as if he were Episcopalian; they have wives and worse. Father Faraday is a good old-fashioned Catholic priest. And insofar as he's a man, what's wrong with having a man around the house?"

I was right against the door now, squatting to make my eye level with the keyhole. There was a long pause in their conversation.

"Mother," the bride said suddenly—with urgency and a noticeable maturity—no longer whining, "if I asked you to follow me somewhere, would you?"

"That depends, Kathleen. What I mean is, of course I would, if it seemed reasonable, but don't you think you'd be better off resting for a few days?—here where there are people to look after you, a familiar environment, the comforts of home . . ."

"No, I don't mean to go away from here, to travel, but you have to promise not to ask any questions, just to go with me."

I was curious myself as to the destination the bride had in mind, although slightly distracted by the pain in my knees, a sensation with which I am well-acquainted, and have, over the years, developed the stamina to endure.

"You are being very mysterious, young lady, but your mother will go along."

"Thank you, oh thank you, Mother, because I discovered just the perfect place while I was having my contractions, and I was afraid it might . . . disappear—I mean I might forget it—just like when you have a dream sometimes that's so vivid and powerful but then you can't remember anything specific the next day, or even an hour later."

I watched the bride splay her legs; she spread them as far, it seemed, as legs could separate, and farther still—perhaps she had as an adolescent performed the acrobatic maneuver called a split; she might have been a cheerleader—it seemed it must be terribly

MARY CAPONEGRO

uncomfortable but this time she uttered no cries, not a sound, as they, adopting what appeared an exaggerated yoga position, crept inside, one after the other, to be embraced by those contours which are even in the imagination, forbidden to the man who inhabits, as vocation, a chamber of secrets. I heard them twice removed now, as if underwater.

"I must admit I feel a bit uneasy here, Kathleen; would you do me the favor of telling me where we are?"

"Well, it's hard to say exactly where, but I can tell you how I found it. In the excruciating and terribly lonely pain of labor, when all of me was opened up, I felt almost delirious, and yet very . . . present, painfully connected to what was happening, and in between contractions I just decided I should be able to inhabit that space myself, in a soothing way; a therapeutic way, I guess you could call it. Shouldn't the haven we give others be available for us too? Doesn't that seem right to you, Mama? Anyway, suddenly I was in a place I'd never known but wanted to come back to, and when I saw you now, I knew I had to bring you with me. I'm very glad you agreed to come." The two women had no suspicion that they were in some fashion exposed to the practiced ear of the man whose profession is to listen through a membrane to all the world's secrets.

"No one would ever think to look for us here."

"I suppose you're right, dear. But what if someone should need either of us? I don't feel right to be unavailable. We do have company, after all. I've always prided myself on being a perfect hostess."

"But mother, we've only just arrived. Stay a while. Besides, it's only fair I reciprocate," the bride said, after a brief pause. My first journey in this world was through a room just like this, that you guided me through. Then somehow we grew estranged from one another."

"You make it all sound a bit tragic, Kathleen, when we've been having such a pleasant, such an interesting visit. I really don't know what you are referring to. And might I suggest you consider the word estrangement in relation to your own son and husband? But you always take offense when I try to remind you of your responsibilities, even though my only concern is your happiness."

"Oh yes, let's not get into it, Mother, I didn't mean anything by it. I love being here with you where it's so embracing, yet expansive too, as if it might extend beyond infinity."

"Such a lovely way of putting it; you are your mother's daughter, aren't you? And I will certainly come again, if I'm invited. If nothing else, it's educational. It shows me just how much we have in common."

It seemed their session had terminated but it was hard to assess, something of the sensation one has during an overseas phone conversation: its disorienting static and delays in transmission of sound.

"Is this the exit, honey?"

"You go first, Mama."

Mrs. Callahan's next words were clearly articulated; no longer did they sound submerged, murky, as I watched the mesmerizing reemergence of the two women. The bride seemed to turn inside out; I have no other words, as inadequate, as pedestrian as these are; I was reminded of the way certain of nature's creatures shed their skins. The bride was again lying in the bed; indeed she had never stood during the entire expedition, and her mother was back at her side, seated, now dabbing inside the bodice of the bride's dressing gown with a linen cloth.

"My breasts feel so swollen." The daughter's plaintive voice addressed her mother.

"Of course they do; they *are* swollen," the latter replied as she continued to execute the dainty motion with the cloth, the inadequacy of which brought to mind the image of the Dutch boy's finger in the dike.

"It's a pity you destroyed that breast pump, dear; rather reckless of you."

"It was in a moment of passion."

"Ah, yes. Where did you say David went? Not to mention my grandchild."

"To investigate something, I think. I'm not really sure. Things are a bit strained between us, actually."

"No doubt. Well, if we don't do something soon I'm afraid you're going to burst, and we can't have that. There is mess enough around here as it is. I suppose that midwife gave you some lactating stimulant. I've never heard of milk coming in quite this early in such . . . volume. I'm going to have to take matters into my own . . ." She hesitated, looked uncharacteristically tentative, for clearly she lacked a destination or function for the parts of herself to which her ellipsis metaphorically alluded. As her voice trailed off, I saw Mrs. Callahan gently, furtively affix her mouth to her daughter's breast, to relieve it of the nourishment meant for another which burdened it so. The bride winced. "Could you try to be gentler, Mother?" she asked. "They're a bit tender, since this is the first time."

The bride's mother obligingly removed her lips from the darkened protuberance no longer veiled by white fabric. She awaited permission as an accompanist awaits the signal from another instrumentalist to initiate music, so as to create, all the more precisely, unity of sound and feeling.

And when that signal came, and she lowered again her head to grasp with her lips what hands would not be useful for, a stream of pale white squirted out, startling us all. I nearly toppled over but repositioned to correct myself, careful to utter no sound. The bride's mother also made adjustments; she appeared to take a deep breath and then, after one unsuccessful attempt, arrested the stream. With enviable dexterity, she reached, while thus occupied, toward the couple's dressing table to retrieve a crystal bowl, into which she released, in an astoundingly refined fashion, the translucent whitish liquid from her mouth, the latter which she dabbed with the same linen cloth. Ignoring the unimpeded flow, she breathed again, and said, "I only wish I had two mouths." Valiantly she resumed her relief measures, acquiring an almost graceful regimen of intake and release, growing, it seemed to me, increasingly acclimated, mother and daughter both, approaching a state of trance-like serenity.

Now I am an efficient man, as I have said, and it troubled me to think of the ignored twin of the bride's mammae, engorged as it was, unattended. Mrs. Callahan, pragmatic woman that she was, had obviously elected not to attempt a system of alternation, fearing the rhythmic complications of leaking and squirting. It had never occurred to me, until that moment, that a baby might nurse from both a mother's breasts, in careful sequencing. Already today I had learned a great deal, primarily with the aid of sight, the sense that is not usually my instructor. But having thus benefited from observation, was it not my duty, now, to intervene? So often we men of the cloth are accused of being "out of touch" with the pragmatic needs of our parishioners, particularly alienated from the needs of women, and inhabiting a comfortably ethereal realm. I looked into my heart and knew I had to overcome my resistance; sometimes matters far less grand than exorcising demons were well worthy of a priest. Such contact, though it be ostensibly at odds with propriety, and with my own inclinations, would be the gift that I could offer. The analogy of artificial respiration seemed fitting: this sort of detachment, yet commitment and intensity.

I crept into the room, literally, for I would need to remain on my knees—I am well practiced—for this novel process. Neither stirred and I made only the softest sounds.

"I am here." I whispered it so softly that it might have been an angel's voice, or strand of dream. And the bride's gasp was likewise a subterranean response to dreamt image or sensation, when I took into my mouth the darkened mounded center of the aureole, controlling my distress to find it already wet, leaking in fact, all the while that Mrs. Callahan attended its twin. The breast itself was hard, like a boulder, but with a quality of translucence, blue veins protruding through the flesh. I had the unique opportunity to use as visual instruction the template across from me, and let this be my focus, rather than the disconcerting image immediately before me. I was prepared now for the energy with which its contents would gush forth. I moved my lips, and not my teeth, in time with Mrs. Callahan's, and found, by some small miracle, a rhythm that seemed appropriate to Kathleen's needs. Inadvertently I glanced at the crystal bowl to see that within the clearer fluid, resembling white watercolor paint, some globules of fat had collected. I managed to check, at first, an impulse to gag, but after this sight, the taste—for I could not approximate Mrs. Callahan's demure dexterity in spitting out every drop of the substance to make room for more—of the cloyingly sweet liquid overwhelmed me. Already, it took all my concentration to be one with it. But certainly my training should have equipped me with the discipline required to transcend my squeamishness, to put mind and spirit over matter, in order to overcome the body's limitations.

And so I did, offering a silent prayer of thanks. And just as when one engages in physical exercise, and after passing a certain threshold of pain, gains momentum and achieves sustained transcendence, I too felt altogether delivered from my limitations. Such a strange suspension this state was, to be intensely present yet entranced: unique in my adventures as a servant. I felt no impatience whatsoever, only a curiosity as to how long a milk-filled

mother's breast required to empty its contents. My only reference was a single farming experience one summer as a boy, tentatively touching a cow's udder—the farmhand laughing, "That
won't get you anywhere, little feller, ya gotta use some muscle,"
as she squeezed my arm to add emphasis before demonstrating
the far more vigorous maneuvers required to make the milk
squirt into the silver pail. She might, I supposed, be proud of me
now—though the bishop would demand an explanation.

Most unfortunately, the indigestion—which was engen-
dered when I indulged in gluttony over Mrs. Callahan's repast,
followed by hearing the bride's reproach and finally by coming
to the aid of a woman—who happened to be the same as she
who had reproached me—in distress—now welled up in my gut
anew, and I was ashamed of my weakness. Mortal that I was, I
would have to admit my subservience to the body. Such a vast
intake of milk for an unaccustomed adult system was bound to
result in some degree of gastric distress. I thought it best to
absent myself before either woman "awakened," for certainly my
becoming ill would be no contribution to the situation. My gift
would be left unsigned, as it were, and how happy this made me,
for this is the joy of my vocation: to help without ostentation, to
offer subtle assistance without expectation of boast or virtue. We
must give freely even when—especially when—the gift entails
sacrifice; even when we would wish nothing so much as to have
the cup pass from our lips.

It seemed in many ways the opportune time to go. I am
a man of God and I had done what I could for the family. There

were other families: a vast world in need of instruction, and I myself with so much to learn. In some other sense, however, I had just arrived; for my observance of these women, and the unique form of my participation in physiological processes that had remained for the greater part of my life abstract, had been instructive in a way I could not define or assimilate. Feeling thus overwhelmed made me want to flee, and yet I was to an equal degree entranced. Perhaps if I rested here with them, as quiet as I had been all this time, I could become for them a part of their landscape, a part of their life. I had the sense that they had been changed by their visit with each other, as most certainly had I by my covert interaction.

Here the undertaker had no place, it seemed. And my own truths seemed disturbingly incomplete. What could I learn from this? How could I apply these lessons? In so many senses, failure felt the order of the day.

Why, then, could I not pull myself from the room, from the sight of the two women, one of with whom I had had particular and unprecedented carnal interaction, for which I had no reference and lacked all vocabulary. I wished her to regain normal consciousness; felt, in fact, that I kept vigil to it—and yet it was this very transformed appearance that mesmerized me—for I am a man of ritual, am I not, performing every day again and again an invisible transformation of the ordinary into the extraordinary: bread into body, bread into body, but that body seen only in mind. Was my nausea and near-vertigo perhaps my own body's excuse to remain?—weakness a catalyst for instruction: address

70 ~~

MARY CAPONEGRO

your ignorance, servant, in order to better be that which you were meant? Humble yourself before the creatures made of Adam's rib, made of man, but who themselves make men?

I myself had seen the process; participated, in some sense, in its perpetuation—though all my efforts likely misinterpreted as thwarting. From sacred texts, from prayer and from my superiors, had come my instruction in the past, but where was I now led? As they reclined, I too would recline, but apart from the bed, here in the corner, where I could witness, but not disturb; reflect upon the role I had played in their sustained interaction. Instinctively I took out my pen: "My children, ladies and gentlemen, good people,"— I put a line through each in turn—"brothers and sisters in Christ"—all addresses seemed prosaic, formulaic—"I would ask that you reflect today on something rather esoteric, something challenging and perhaps initially off-putting. Christian responsibilities are far more complex than they first appear, than we might have learned through the catechism lessons of our youth. Consider me, if you would, a kind of . . . midwife, who mediates collectively your birth in Christ, your baptism into new life. You must remind yourselves, should you ever feel mistrustful toward me, that my sole purpose on this earth is to assist you, as your servant."

No sooner had I penned the words than I began to feel some mitigation of the turbulence within my bowels. Realizing that these were indeed the means through which I could calm myself and my digestion, I proceeded with the outline for my homily.

THE SON'S
BURDEN

⇝ "Beans have been known to sprout inside the bowel," says my eccentric, self-schooled sister, "therefore nothing is impossible." She says it with authority, yet casually, as other individuals might say, unprompted, "lovely afternoon" or "care for coffee?" "Will it rain?" She does not vocalize, however, the sentence's denouement, which all in range of hearing tacitly supply: "even the prospect of Brother succeeding." This is her own peculiar way of bolstering Father's confidence in me, urging him to renew the lease of tolerance and expectation, whose expiration might in fact far better serve me. This is her way.

Beans have been known to sprout in the bowel; indeed, I take her word on this. It is as conceivable as every other anatomical curiosity she enshrines. I endorse these haricots emigres, but for reasons far more elemental than can be inferred from Sister's twisted syllogism. I am an inventor, or as Father might amend, an ever-aspiring one, and thus a traitor to my vocation were I not to second "nothing is impossible." One thing grafted onto another— a griffin, or a sphinx with a ram's head; my calling is to expand the imagination, for an inventor, it is said, possesses vision that his neighbors likely lack. Yet that which others take for granted is to him opaque: "Ring in the new," for example—cursed universal slogan that is, in my view, far less "fathomable" than my eventual success, less credible than the existence of a cryosphinx.

"Ring in the new," we are annually instructed in the all too familiar collective exhortation, but something rings false in my ear when I, repeatedly, am recipient of the flaccid greeting, "Happy New Year!" Does this trite formula do justice to the mix of trepidation and relief that marks the close of one collection of regrets and the promiscuous proliferation of an entirely new set of vacuous promises? Round again we go, one might more accurately say: the ineluctable disguised as marvel, and yet our rituals, no matter be they made of air or straw, appear to comfort. Familiarity cushions the blow of transition; tradition ensconces novelty. And I, Thomas Edward Smalldridge (invention in hand, or more precisely, in pocket), am once again in the parlor with Father and Sister, a triad augmented this year by my fiancée—enduring together the ritual for which no amount of narration could prepare the one not bound by blood, and for which all explanation is irrelevant to the one thereby ligated for all time.

Each of these good ladies (including the absent one, who presides upstairs) may console in her way, even while offering unwitting challenge to my equanimity, but I am grateful all the same for being buffered from my father. By what, or whom, I am buffered is of course another matter, and a story in itself: the story of my sister, which is more or less in equal parts, the story of my mother, and of my father—a story which in telling would

MARY CAPONEGRO

likely garner incredulity if not distaste, and so in responsibility to my fiancée I must expose myself, I must show firsthand that to which no mere telling could do justice.

Eleanor is my sole sibling; eternally, it would appear, spinster, though one mysterious thwarted suitor figures ambiguously in our family history: a well-to-do physician whose practice is no longer near and of whom we seldom speak. The extent to which she thinks of him I am not privileged to know. I do, however, know that Eleanor is erratically sympathetic to my particular plight, akin to her own: how to transcend this Smalldridge "new" year ritual and all that it connotes, to achieve what is ideally, truly, our destiny—unless rising be not in our future, and destiny already in our midst, not in the least inscrutable. And if destiny be already at our feet, it seems reasonable to suppose that no matter how vigorously or frequently we might pick them up, they will yield us no motion other than running-in-place; thus stasis remains our legacy: the proverbial animal chasing its tail— somehow less nobly tragic than Sisyphus and his trusty appendage. Do I digress? Father would say I do, habitually, at times supplanting continuity altogether. Nonetheless I carry on.

Ever since I found egress from mother's womb—in fact, even before—my sister has made my welfare (or more accurately, my struggle) her preoccupation. My sister does not blame me for what she perceives as my incompetence, my failure, my . . . deformity if you will. I am in her eyes incapable of being other than incapable. And this she attributes to the repeated gestures of excess that were threaded through mother's pregnancy and my infancy: a reckless weaving and unweaving of resilient stationary strands on a golden loom with golden crown. These are precisely the accoutrements of my childhood; this image as much to me my mother as the actual woman. Since I could utter, no, even prior to speech, I beheld that statuesque form with abundant— one might even say effulgent—golden hair gathered up atop her noble, shapely head, yet nonetheless cascading over her forehead and temples, uncontainable; her body stayed by a golden frame, with elbows aloft, and her arms spinning air. She would nightly place the regal instrument between her thighs, then initiate the intricate collaboration of foot and hand that has held me in thrall since childhood, releasing and engaging the pedals while gracefully plucking the strings to produce vibration. It became for me a golden loom, then a golden shield, and then a ship's sail against the glow of a golden sun, and so on and so on and so on. It produced in her young son's imagination a marriage of ship and bicycle. From this memory and its inspiration I made, at an early age, a drawing and later a model I called the kitecycle (which in my mind mimicked the "double action pedaling" of her harp). It was essentially a bicycle, but equipped with additional buoyancy, so that on a gusty day, one riding might be simultaneously of this earth and above it. (Later versions included a failed attempt to model the wheel's spokes on harp strings, so that one might "pluck and ride" or alternate the two activities.) My mother has told me that when she lay with me in utero, she played to soothe me and prepare me for my journey from the womb. And yet,

MARY CAPONEGRO

according to my sister, the physicians assigned her to strictest bed rest, instructing her to engage in no excess movement until she delivered me, and they would have indubitably regarded this flagrant choreography of limbs a reckless transgression of her gravid state and thus potential violation of my safety. My sister insists that not only was I damaged, incapacitated by my mother's self-indulgence and intransigence, but that her siren's song continues to distort my brain, my will. I hear, I obey, I melt, become stupid, bemused, addled, malleable, mesmerized, paralyzed; I become, in short, my sister says, my mother's son. What can I offer to this accusation but a resigned shrug: so be it, if I am so, or am more so than an "average" boy; whose son would I be if not my mother's? I am the one it was my destiny to be, although my father claims that I dishonor him, in fact eschew my destiny.

LADIES AND GENTLEMEN: THE HARP HEADBOARD
Admittedly, the headboard is of an unusual shape, not rectangular. Moreover, the wooden spindles to which we are accustomed have been replaced by finer ones, of wire or gut. These spindle-strings preserve the sense of verticality, against the sensuous sweep that now supplants the horizontal; for the inventor knows intuitively the solace a horizon line implies, particularly when we, like the sun, lay down our bodies to rest; the inventor understands the uneasiness created by relinquishing that linearity.

Eleanor and I have spent more than two decades together in this house—she nearly three—and are more intimate in each other's ways than with any other being, and yet she remains in certain ways a stranger, more precisely an enigma, for Sister makes communication something quite unorthodox, unsettling (it may be the combined effect of utterance and appearance, as she has inherited the preternatural brightness and amplitude of Mother's eyes, yet not, alas, the pulchritude; whereas one feels invited, summoned by the beacon of the latter, by the former one is over and over again startled—eyes so wide and so wide-set as to be unseemly, like the open eyes of the dead). Concerning communication, I suppose one cannot blame the girl, for what have we to speak about but Father, and that which derives from Father, and who could more than subsist on such monotonous fare: nutrition devoid of delectation.

> But what is reaped in return is well worth that sacrifice, ladies and gentlemen, for the curving headboard is prerequisite to the recumbent figure's opportunity to be in a soothing limbo between repose and activity. Though supine, she can position herself in any number of postures beside these delicate vertical spindles and occupy her hands fully while the rest of her body is in repose. Only her arms need do the bending—unless she prefers to approximate the sitting position traditional to a seated player. For those without the energy to support the weight of the instrument, this allows a more casual, even idle, plucking or strumming from one side only, so as not to have to relinquish altogether contact with the beloved instrument. Thus, a valetudinarian could remain, to some degree, in practice.

Even before recession severed him from his beloved railroad, Father felt increasingly compelled to craft his leisure—what leisure he possessed—into something edifying, and now makes instruction even of festivity. As was the case throughout our upbringing, he offers lessons whose form is intended to build our character, while the content is principally for my benefit, so as to seed success (no matter how far-fetched a notion my success, at this point, might be). For I am, after all, the son, and furthermore, in Father's eyes as well as Sister's, Mother's son, thus all the more in need of guidance and discipline.

This then is the reason for the charts by which I am surrounded, the maps Cecilia gazes at with misguided fascination (no doubt imagining the pins with which they are riddled to indicate exotic places we have visited, rather than the "sacred sites" from which invention sprung), even the plethora of mismatched furnishings representing the entire history of furniture and appliances, an aesthetics solely educative. On the lists that greet us at the vestibule, we must match columns of inventions to reveal influences, predecessors: lathe with apple corer, drill with eggbeater, Gothic swing bench with adjustable railroad seat; but the dolphin image opposite the toilet is obviously a trick: a different breed of analogy. It would require a pupil even more stubborn than myself to botch the preliminary drill. (Among my earliest, murkiest memories, I recall an additional toilet training hurdle: when Mother was at harp and Father thus in charge, I had to hold it in until I somehow named the mammal decorating the fashionable eighties toilets: hence my first words included Mama, Papa,

Nora, Dolphin!) But there are many new hurdles to cross between now and midnight, when my invention is to be presented.

> *In time, the ornate headboard might become a sought-after furnishing; even in a nonmusical household, it suggests opulence, grandeur. Louis XIV might covet such a bed. What more lively conversation piece could grace a guest room? Instead of singing oneself to sleep, there is the option of playing oneself to sleep. And if one wished to announce one's wakefulness at daybreak, to servants or caretakers or relatives, the Harp-Bed allows a far more decorous alternative than shouting or ringing a pedestrian bell: a celestial summons, if you will.*

How all this began is something known only to Thomas and Eleanor, Julia and Hubert; how this upbringing distinguishes itself from those of others, or from what it might have been, is not our privilege to know, as we observe it with bias. But not every story need be objective, and so I have tried to tell—until telling's futility revealed itself to me—to her whom I would wed, how ABC took on a form that was uniquely—might one even say perversely?—Smalldridge.

One's formal education generally includes the sequence of our nation's presidents, the capitals of states, multiplication tables, spelling bees, geography and science quizzes. These, however, are inadequate models for our family education; there is no question that the rigor of the latter outstripped one-hundred-fold the former. Ironically, despite the renowned university of which our windy city boasts (not to mention Mother's dream of sending son and daughter both to the esteemed Sorbonne), a college education was not, as they say, in the cards, for Thomas or Eleanor Smalldridge. I could not claim to be deprived, as I too can trace Hoover, F.D.R., etc. back to Washington; spell Mississippi backward without blinking an eye or squeezing an *s* (and then provide its capital); identify igneous rock or cumulus cloud; compute 9 x 8 or 5 x 12 without a pause; parse any complex English sentence; converse ebulliently, albeit with limited vocabulary, in French (at least with Mother); no, our quarrel is less about our education's lack than its surfeit—and its specificity, for it was neither general nor liberal.

For example, as recreation to pass the hours during journeys and rainy days of our youth, my sister and I were permitted to play (as carefree as we were to be in all our lives) a common children's game. "I packed my trunk and in it I put" was the reprise, and this game's goal was the accrual of the entire alphabet in objects—rendered only verbally, of course, with players alternating letters. The Smalldridge version deviated from the standard game in this respect: the alphabetized contents of our verbal baggage were confined to one category—inventions. It began innocently enough, but evolved over time, under Father's tutelage, into a version far more stringent, whereby we were enjoined to exhaust the alphabet repeatedly until no invention was left unuttered. I'd volley with my sister: abacus, brake, cogwheel, digging stick (how lovely were those occasions when a phrase within a phrase could be achieved, when I'd supply a random *a* and Sister would relate a *b*, as in the simple case of *arrow, bow)*. How pleased we were, when within Father's strictures we could fashion private amusement. These self-contained pairings were our sibling's spelling bond, though Father soon enough discouraged them.

With Mother, between her practice sessions, the game was modified: "Let's tinker, shall we, Tommy? Don't tell Hubert." I was charmed to be her co-conspirator, but fearful, lest we be found out. She modified the game to target names of composers (sometimes we dwelled for hours in *b*); then key signatures, i.e., pieces written in the key of that letter; then forms, from arabesques, bagatelles, etudes, to impromptus, mazurkas, nocturnes, to polonaises, rondos, sonatas, closing with waltzes. But if we could not immediately find a category for a letter, we either skipped it or invented one; we were not vexed. And when I later proposed a more refined—indeed restricted—version, which combined categories, e.g. all pieces in *B♭* by Beethoven, she smiled, then sighed, and said, "but already it's less lighthearted, isn't it, Thomas, dear," stroking my cheek, laying aside her harp to favor me with her lap—"making it so rigid, it is a game after all. Save that energy and discipline for technique: scales, arpeggios, exercises. The pianist who warms up with Beethoven instead of Hannon or Czerny is bound to stumble and will never rhapsodize. Wouldn't you cringe to hear a harpist performing sloppy, uneven, broken chords? Who would care to listen to a flautist who ignored his embouchure?" Her rigor never unalloyed by play, she then commenced with "eensy weensy spider" to

MARY CAPONEGRO

remind me of my earliest "lessons," when she had guided my hand across the strings to supervise the execution of arpeggios. ("See Mama's daddy-longlegs fingers? Here, follow them. Tommy has a spider hand if he wants, too.") Many such learning games she invented for my engagement—my tiny hand now larger, guided by hers, crawling over coated threads, then incorporating the actual notes of the tune. By the time E.W. had crawled "up the spout again," I had been cajoled, distracted from whatever child's misery discontented me in the first place. (If Sister's assertion is to be believed, that a spider's spun silk is five times the strength of steel, then Mother's analogy is all the more cogent: a web with the tensile strength to sustain repeated plucking.)

I did not confide to Eleanor this next small game. True to her playful nature, Mother fashioned a comparison between the shortest strings that sounded forth the highest notes, and what she referred to as my "short hairs," the fringe at my nape she gently pulled to tickle me after she brushed my hair. "My daughter," she would complain rhetorically (I was too young to appreciate the tone of bitter grief) "will not let me brush her hair. She says she prefers the snarls to the touch of my hand. Imagine that! How severe she looks with it always wound on top of her head—it only calls attention to her widow's peak. It hasn't been the style for years. Imagine a girl not caring to have her mother comb her hair!" On other days she cited other denials—but who was I then, so young, to plead with my sister to relent—meanwhile the instrument and I continued to exchange the privilege of her lap.

Each year the game advanced—and does still!—in difficulty, as father challenged us not only to exploit the alphabet in a general fashion, but to restrict our sources historically as well: inventions of the ancient Greeks and Romans, for example—the preceding months spent in preparation so as to be equipped to surrender in antiphonal sequence with no hiatus: Archimedean screw, bucket chain hoist, and so on, or auger, brace, and countersinker, donkey mill, frame saw, and gimlet. Our inadvertent elision of *e* insured that we would do twenty *e* inventions as penance, the ancients' contributions now off-limits as further penance, and so we moved in time—INVENTIONS OF THE MEDIEVAL PERIOD: adze, brace, carving knife, demountable table, faldstool . . . skidding to a premature halt at his booming admonition, "You skipped the *e!*" Each time we overlooked it, we had to begin again with a new set of strictures. Perhaps unconsciously I practiced a self-sabotage, spontaneously aborting at the fifth letter to keep the *h* at bay, knowing even early on that Mother's precious instrument, or any version of it, was not a worthy candidate. (Was it his curse to have his first name and her harp both begin with *h?* I am surprised, in retrospect, he did not change it. "YOU MAY NOT SKIP A LETTER. YOU ARE RESPONSIBLE FOR E.A.C.H. ONE!!!!! Tomorrow give me twenty *e* inventions, inventions of the last decade, then inventions between this new year and last. . . ." Etc. Until completing the punitive list, we were not allowed to engage in any activity containing *e,* to utilize any object containing an *e* or to employ any words containing *e* in speech. So effective was the punishment that I shuddered when I recognized the note so named in passages of music mother played

MARY CAPONEGRO

that day. Father's power was persuasion. One could no longer play off the top of one's head, so to speak, as protracted hesitation invariably incurred Father's wrath, and guaranteed we roll that massive mythic boulder back to square one to start again with fresh inventions: Archimedean screw, bucket chain hoist, and so on; great was our relief when we came toward closure at tread-wheel, and by the time we got to *w* felt we were drawing water from a well so deep it was unfathomable: tenon, undershot water wheel, Vitruvian water wheel; (no, not allowed); quickly we sub-stituted vine dresser's knife and gained permission to pursue the alphabet's few remaining increments: wheel (no, too general), wedge and beam press (acceptable), yoke (no, too general), too long stumped by *y* we had no choice but to be sent back to *h* and lose our progress, plodding wearily again, all the way to *w,* more cautiously, almost to *z,* "please, Papa, pretty please"—my sister and I, in a reckless gesture of giddy playfulness, employed sleep's colloquial symbol in the slot for *z:* its repeated character standing for the reward of repose we would obtain when our alphabet vigil was completed—would not our accomplishment in this sense create sleep and thus legitimately be cited as our invention?—to Father's satisfaction, but he didn't care for the joke, and insisted, despite our tears, that we begin again, again, and again, and thus until dawn after dawn after dawn.

Now, as then, there is no room on our calendars for dates as nor-mal families might record; the ones considered here reflect a record of the past, rather than anticipation of the future: no birthdays, anniversaries, excursions. Instead, our calendars are customized, capacious enough to accommodate every invention's date of birth, as well as the inventor's—both day and year of its patenting. Thus this nascent year, nineteen hundred thirty-two, serves as a base from which we extrapolate, backward, to all the years preceding. (Failing to fill the page with ink, what's more with evenly distributed ink—ensuring that each day's box contains at least one item—or incorrectly labeling a box, disqualifies us, for our greetings to him are based on these protocols.) While an average father might balk if a son failed to call him Sir, my sister and I are found disrespectful if we do not greet him by the specificity of the day in its relation to the history of invention and discovery (for instance, happy anaphylaxis, happy Bunsen burner, happy cotton gin). "Oh happy moldboard plow, Deere!" we crooned to each other, to link inventor with device: private jokes that were desperate mnemonics. But under no circumstances would I presume to offer Mother's instrument in any guise, whether the version by Erard or by Pleyel, whether cross-strung or double-action, whether Egyptian, French, or Irish, because any mention of those contributions would be negated automatically: "There is no such thing," my father has ever averred, "as a HAPPY HARP!"

All of the aforementioned activities serve as routine preparation, leading to the annual marathon event, which itself is meant to culminate in the unveiling of my "latest" invention. Our ritual exchange takes the following form: first he toasts us—with some festive surrogate for alcohol, or occasionally bootlegged liquor—

and bids us make new in this new year. This is our challenge, our signal. We stand.

Sister always "serves," so to speak, leaving me the responsibility of returning the ball, but the content of the serve is in fact our collaboration. This is possible because our language bears the symmetry that siblings' speaking can (and stranger still for being Smalldridge), and because my sister wishes nothing so much as to boost the chances of my success.

"Indeed, fill your glass, Father," she chimes in response, as she has always done at this early evening hour of December thirty-first, for all the years that have led up to and including this year nineteen hundred thirty-one. (Why does the rhyme of day and year unnerve me?—as if the month should add a *one* to be their unlucky inversion of *thirteen*.) "Fill it and ring in the new." Then she continues with the opening we have rehearsed: "Embrace it, lest it come after you surreptitiously, stealthily, to have its way with you, lest it jangle its bells and blow its crude horn in your face and scatter a cloud of deceptively colorful currency that must later be gathered bit by bit from the floor on your knees." (Who but I could know the destination of her ever-elliptical speech, even had I not participated in its composition.) My fiancée's gnarled brow preoccupies me, and I can hardly afford the distraction. Unacquainted with my sister, and this most peculiar ritual, she no doubt finds the phrases ominous (as I—now to my sudden shame—intended, when composing it, long before I knew it would be heard by anyone but "family"). To the uninitiated, the occasion is necessarily at odds with expectation. But, true to character, she whispers only praise: "Thomas, how impressive that your family lets the woman make the toast." Many conventions are unraveled on this occasion, in this family, my Cecilia, my innocent Cecilia. I will have my say soon enough. Eleanor then winks at me and says softly "although far more likely it is I with trolley and brush to the floor at a later hour"—my clue!—"restoring the appearance of order in the aftermath of celebration. For I am in effect the woman of the house, am I not, Father?"

And then we as always begin our ordeal in earnest: "What is your sister talking about, Thomas?" At his prompt, I begin to parrot back the proper answers: I tell him the name he seeks is *suction sweeper* . . . descended from what cleans the streets. "And while you're at it, Tom, why don't you tell us how it came into existence, and how it has changed between then and now?"

Mercifully, I am prepared. "The carpet sweeper paved the way, if you will."

"I will not," my father interrupts, always eager for the opportunity to mock my speech—and wasn't I the fool to mix a metaphor early on in my presentation. Of course he would not brook my melding of the machine that cleans, indoors, by suction, with a verb that could imply cement, asphalt, etc.: all ingredients of pavement.

"I was sloppy, Father." I amend, "the carpet sweeper was the suction sweeper's immediate ancestor." I explain dutifully that D.T. Kenney's was the first and basic patent for both fixed and portable vacuum cleaners. But I should have preceded this with

MARY CAPONEGRO

the citation, in particular, of the stationary vacuum cleaner for residences, which had suction pump and dust separator in cellar. In an effort to compensate, I omit no relevant anecdotal detail, citing all dates and figures: the 1917 Montgomery Ward catalog's twelve-pound portable vacuum, for example—very popular at $14.95. But of course my omission will not escape him. Despite its being out of sequence now, I must report that in 1859 the pure suction type was patented; and in 1860, the trolley unit with suction and brush action. I conclude, flustered, that only two years ago, ninety-five percent of all vacuums owned in households were light portable units.

My sister distracts me with an exaggerated mimed gesture, her hand at her throat, her mouth unbecomingly agape. I know I have been sloppy, it takes me time to get my bearings; must she call attention to my omission? My bemusement produces further silent drama: her head thrown forward in staccato motions that suggest spasm. What now, Eleanor, what now? (The seating arrangement is hardly ideal—How could it be, with every resting place a haphazard museum piece?—Cecilia directly across from Eleanor; too late to rectify that. What was I thinking? I wasn't. Not about bodies in space certainly.)

As always, I am slow-witted under the vise that is Father's stare; his tiny piercing nicotine-colored eyes appear the inverse of Mother's, Sister's. Sister begins to cough, and my fiancée moves to rise—to flee, I presume, who could blame her?—and then I realize that she is concerned for my sister's welfare, and means rather to pat her on the back, or perhaps fetch her a glass of water. I place my hand gently to restrain her, and wink, only now discerning Sister's code myself—she is reminding me that the British inventor Booth almost choked on his own vacuum experiment on Victoria Street. Unfortunately my intended reassurances to Cecilia produce only greater confusion. Hoping both to clarify for my alarmed fiancée, and fulfill my student-duties, I articulate the forgotten fact. (How Sister and I loved to play-act an embellished version of this event in our youth—she taking the role of the gagging inventor, I the role of the horrified maître d', then exchanging. "Sir, sir, what ever are you doing to our expensive pink plush dining chair? The food and drink we offer should be sufficient, you need not imbibe the plush seat! Sir, would you care for a straw?") How rude a noise we could produce when playing the inventor was our goal and our delight, but this aspect was reserved, of course, for our private play, that which was unsupervised; for while Father rode the rails—ironically the Adamson Act that eventually limited his workday to no more than eight hours made our particular child labor more excessive—we studied independently, to be tested upon his return. When the games were executed under Father's scrutiny, all recreation vanished. (Exactitude, he chanted daily, is the inventor's most efficient tool.) The historical incident involving Booth is not, today, required by Father to be demonstrated. No props are demanded. I am spared. Perhaps Sister's incipient pantomime has been sufficient.

Nor does her prompting earn me demerits, since Father knows it gives her pleasure. (And he humors her, as he refuses to humor me, knowing that she imagined her clue was unde-tected by any but its intended recipient.) My fiancée seems slightly dazed. How could she be otherwise? The only conso-lation is that her lack of awareness precludes reinforcement of my humiliation.

But she is kind. She would not, I think, judge me for my lack. My Cecilia is forgiving; she is a veritable fountain of clemency. I have seen her demonstrate the utmost generosity to strangers, to beggars, even stray dogs and cats, as well as relatives and friends. Did we not first meet on a charity call she made to our house?—a visit I did not permit her to repeat until tonight, for obvious and awkward reasons—when she went door to door through our purlieus of the city, asking that we maintain a link in conscience to the residual urban dwellers: those citizens, says Cecilia, that did not have the privilege of seeking new horizons, greener pastures, an embrace of yews! Was I not instantly struck by the benevolence, charm, and candor of this handsome woman who would have every cause to stay within the confines of her own luxurious Oak Park residence, gazing in her bedroom mir-ror the day long at the amber luster of her hair and eyes, basking in the light and warmth and spaciousness an infamous architect created, commissioned by her father.

How much the opposite of my own abode, where it seems the clutter was not quite so overwhelming until five years ago, when Father bought the u.s. Patent Office's odds and ends at auction—their loss our gain, but their gained space our loss.(Such is the liability of an irresistible bargain.) Moreover, the

Patent Office's desperate purge in order to make room for new inventions allowed Father to enhance his educational arsenal at rock-bottom prices and yet consider the purchase an act of charity supporting his favorite cause. (My father's notion of charity is rather more specialized than my fiancée's.)

Yes, I, despite the encumbrances of my upbringing, have chosen well, and thoughtfully, but will I be rewarded with requital? How can Cecilia forgive this crude package in which my life is wrapped?—as poignantly and distastefully caparisoned as a fetus bound to its mother's stool? (Sister insists this image is authentic in obstetric lore.) That is the question, in a test much more demanding even than the one I must habitually undergo at Father's hands; for I intend to profit from my elder sister's aborted engagement, by not repeating her mistake (the details of which will remain ever veiled). If I were fortunate enough to have a ring to present I would leave no opportunity for that ring to come full circle and like a boomerang, return to me. All deem my every invention an error, but this is one fundamental mistake I intend to avoid. (At this confession I must also admit my presumptuousness in titling her, *fiancée,* who is in fact, until a ring is secured, technically *fiancée-to-be.*)

The first step, obviously, is to obtain a ring, my options unfortunately limited to gaining a favor from either Sister or Father. My expectations vacillate between labeling this on the one hand a Herculean challenge, and on the other, a foregone conclusion. Practitioners of my vocation would seem to have triumphed over the Herculean—does not setting the city of

MARY CAPONEGRO

Chicago on stilts seem a worthy contemporary version of redirecting a river through the Augean stables? So why should not I, an inventor, be equal to the task? Much has been accomplished in our time that weeks before its execution would have been deemed mythic or fantastic. Somehow I must manufacture a pause, and signal or query Eleanor in private. I must gain her sympathy. This is feasible, it seems to me, for Sister is in support of me, fundamentally (as I have stated), despite occasionally distorted expression of her affection.

For instance, Eleanor would claim, vituperatively, that Mother's habitual absence until the time of the New Year's unveiling, demonstrates her indifference to our situation. But lacking interpretive skills, Sister cannot understand the coded signals of reassurance that I, albeit with considerable concentration, can recognize. (She has, in short, no ear.) As she has never learned to play an instrument or listen critically, never developed the ability to distinguish one historical period from another or identify a composer's stylistic signature, she interprets all sound that emanates from mother's chamber as one incessant, superficial reverie. And yet she also accuses Mother of flaunting her technique. I, on the other hand, am privileged to know that in this moment, Mother senses our distress, and offers soothing medieval compositions: simple lute-like sonorities that foster calm and concentration. Abandoning the technical bravado often showcased in the period of her specialty, and for that matter, in the compositions for her instrument in general, she substitutes the meditative for the virtuosic.

All this is lost on poor Eleanor, who, doubly impoverished, lacks access to the treasure of aesthetic edification that was my privilege. She did not care to accompany Mother and me to the Oriental Institute—surely she must have been invited, as the elder, smarter child—thus, here our otherwise tandem learning forked, and she repaired to the furthest outposts of the body, with even greater assiduity than we demonstrated in the study of invention. (Perhaps Dr. Cranshaw was impressed, years later, at the boldness of such study in a woman; or perhaps initially intrigued and then repelled, or perhaps he made incorrect assumptions regarding what this fervent—if eccentric—scholarship implied. This remains my sister's secret, upon which no amount of research can shed light.)

But I am privy to abundant secrets. Mother has taken me to the great Louvre upon her lap, where ensconced in her embrace, I found her descriptions of the art housed in the redoubtable museum as magnificent as the artifacts themselves. The *Winged Victory* of Samothrace does not preside over my imagination, though I saw it at a tender age. (Mother tells me she did not dare leave me at home again since Sister had once severely reproved her for doing so.) But harp images that a viewer might merely glance at compel me unto death. Equally ensorcelling was her recitation of harp-related literary passages, most notably what served for me as Ur-text: the paragraph in which Frédéric, aboard ship with Mme. Arnoux—who will later become his lover—honors her reverie by rewarding the long-haired harpist whose music—"an eastern romance, all about daggers, flowers, and stars"—elicited it.

Of course he gave that coin, I thought, the moment I first heard my mother read it (and each time I have reread it on my own). I would give my whole fortune, if I possessed one, in such an instance (just as I would have Cecilia on that first day, for her cause). But alas, to my shame, I have not even the equivalent of the gold louis that Flaubert's Frédéric gave. If I did, I might honor that same instrument in a unique and modern way (a way to which I alone aspire). And yet, if someone were to offer me exchange: my memory of the passage for the gold, those sentences cut out of every copy of the Frenchman's novel for a thousand times their weight in gold, I would refuse. I would never barter this passage, whose value to me could—and I am certain would—be dismissed in a single adjective, by him who would have me educated in a fashion antithetical to the sentimental. (As to my sister, when I tried to share the sentiment, she offered nothing but the tale of a Comedie-Francais actress who was known to bend coins with her hands.)

But who am I to expect such consolations?—I who have peered into paintings by Rembrandt and Rubens and Dürer, as much to scrutinize the various representations of King David, harp in hand, as to admire the masters' techniques. King David's image on the ivory cover of Dagulf's Psalter was our first stop at the actual Louvre, and it eclipsed for me the *Mona Lisa*'s enigmatic smile. Similarly, the sensuous and meticulous angels of Van Eyck and Fra Angelico were most compelling to me for the instruments they carried. Staring intently at the lacquered surface of a fifth-century Greek vase on which a harp-playing

muse is depicted, I perceived such a portrait as would be worthy of my mother.

And even now, I, who profess to accept the cryosphinx's existence, am naturally receptive to the sight of a griffin's paws holding
what instrument but a harp, carved in relief on the capital of
Canterbury Cathedral, seen by me, at a tender age, in a photograph.

Oh Father, is not the harp as old as the oldest inventions produced by humankind, an instrument whose history is ancient
in its dignity? Is it not the centerpiece of the earliest civilizations? But memory's rose perforce does not lack thorns.
Consider, for example, the limestone relief from the Palace of
Nineveh of 650 B.C.: I could draw for you the angular harp
played by an attendant of the king and queen. I could trace the
tree which bears within its uppermost, finger-like branches, the
severed head of the late ruler of Elam, just above the king and
queen, oblivious or disinterested, dining en plein air, thus serenaded. That same thorned bloom grows abundant in later land-
scapes as luxuriant as *The Garden of Earthly Delights* by
Hieronymous Bosch, whose sensual chaos I combed incessantly,
enchanted, playing the game my mother had devised for me to
make a child's museum visits less tedium than fun. The game,
of course, was to find the harp. And so I did, sifting through
dense imagery to discover in the painting's far right an instrument quite unlike those played by Renaissance angels, and in
quite different relation to the nude figure who seemed to be, if
anything, played *by* the hybrid harp/dulcimer/lute toward

MARY CAPONEGRO

which he faced, and which might as easily have been a crucifix. I sensed an ominous abandon, as if behind the instrument's association with placidity, lurked a subtler and thus all-the-more disquieting suggestion of violence. Might I have asked Mother to resolve these tortured perceptions? I would not have wished to sully her enthusiasm or worry her, or tarnish the purity of the vision which was for her, it seemed to me, pure gold. Help me solve this mystery, Cecilia, of how the harp in heaven finds itself one day the harp in hell! Help me, because my memory is littered irrevocably with harps that take the shape of bows, of crescents, of ladles, spoons; harps that are sculpture or picture or merely the art of themselves: their elaborate ornamented forepillar painted or blossoming into a sphinx or what Sister would consider a tumescence. Help me, because instead of golden crowns atop these glorious forepillars I sometimes see crowned heads decapitated, rolling over verdant fields stained ever after crimson.

But what has this to do, from any objective viewpoint, with a green steatite fragment depicting kilted men with feathers in their hair and bow-shaped harps in hand, or with a crescent painted yellow, turquoise, red and black, culminating in a sphinx-like head, all as precious and delicate as a bracelet? Where is the threat in that? an educated (or should I say conventionally educated) man or woman would ask. In a terra cotta plaque from Ishchali? And I have no concrete answer. A thousand words, as many images, abundant anecdotes, but their accumulation ultimately mute.

It seems innocent enough, does it not, as a child's reward . . . the city's Oriental Institute?—a trip to Montgomery Ward's instrument floor, or in later years, Lyon Healy, to replace a broken harp string, and later still to Wurlitzer's. Up and down Michigan Avenue the two of us would stroll—the glamorous, cultivated mother and devoted, precocious son, and not one shopkeeper or curator or pedestrian knew what manner of instruction "complemented" culture once we returned home.

Nora come and see, come and see the lovely things. Please do come with us next time.

No, Tommy, I'm not wanted there. I'm busy just the same.

Most resonant of all the images was a small Greco-Roman intaglio gem carved with a harpist and dog motif. Who might have guessed that I would someday conjure practical use for this Chalcedony scarab from 500 B.C.? It haunts me now, more than when young, for it is more distinctive than a diamond. If I could procure this milky jewel for Cecilia and set it on a band, it might be as personal and particular as if I had sculpted it myself.

But I would also think, each time I kissed her hand and viewed anew the diminutive depiction: am I, to her, that dog? Am I the stray for whom she plays with such earnest devotion, intent upon healing my dogged life? There are indeed advantages to the conventional: the standard precious diamond set in silver, universal symbol of a vow set in a stone. Yes, all the archeology that unearthed

MARY CAPONEGRO

these ancient artifacts seems less a feat than the procuring of even the most pedestrian jewel for sweet Cecilia's slender finger.

The history of art, insists my father, is not a study for a man; a man should be concerned with actual events that changed men's lives: with wars and armies, treaties, rulers, progress, and machines. A broader history. But how does Father accommodate the legacy of Marie Antoinette, who in balancing a life between her subjects and her instrument, found herself suddenly without a head? (What I cannot bring myself to ask Mother, neither, then, can I ask Father.) I am left to my own devices (literally), and find myself assaulted by unbidden images: the Frenchwoman's head served not on a silver platter like John the Baptist but, in my fantasy, on a harp, perhaps her very own, held sideways by six attendants, exhibiting the ceremony of those carrying a coffin. These images have been kept alive in my imagination, because they don't and never will adorn the Smalldridge parlor walls, but they reside with me, supplementing, internally, portraits and cartography, graphs and charts.

That which was my earthly heaven (and in which art not my Father) was this simple game of *find the harp,* more enticing to a child's sensibility than Father's instructional games.

And why must finding solace or encouragement be less rewarding an endeavor than this game Mother created? Why couldn't it be as simple and as thrilling, to, for instance, *find the ring* in Sister's chamber, *find the YES* in Father's stern demeanor, or, for that matter, *find the new* approach to executing my (apparently preposterous) ideas, or, finally, *find the will* to turn away from all these years of futile effort! Granted, the new invention I am to present at midnight is objectively no more likely to elicit approval than all its predecessors, despite my desperate, fervent hopes. But whose right is it to deem one worthy of love and the seeking of love? None but that love's object, I would think. And so I blurt out to my sister, much more abruptly than I intended, "Eleanor, I wish to marry"—and then whisper, before Father or Cecilia can take notice, "but have no ring."

THE PAGE–TURNING FAN

The dedicated musician must practice in every season; and each season, as all instrumentalists know, has its tribulations. Humidity in excess or dearth is the enemy of all instruments (particularly those that feature strings!). And need I mention the inevitable instability of tuning that results from seasons changing? The craftsmen of our own windy city of Chicago helped create a harp better suited to the sterner seasons, and I introduce an addition to these advances—for how could a musician wear gloves while playing or wave a paper fan to stir the air, with no free hand?

Observe. The harpist is fatigued from the heat, perspiring, uncomfortably warm. Moreover she needs all her strength to continue playing, and can spare no energy to turn pages at crucial moments: transitions, climaxes, accelerando passages. The Page-Turning Fan solves both problems in a single—excuse the pun—blow. The harpist is refreshed, perspires less, and she does not need to perform gratuitous gestures. The additional coordination required to turn a page between challenging passages is more than she

MARY CAPONEGRO

should be required to possess. How could it be effected grace-
fully? Of all musicians, the harpist has the greatest obliga-
tion to grace, for through folklore and art, her image as angel
is fixed in our imagination.

But Tommy, how do you know the page that turns will be the right one?
And how will you ensure that it is only one rather than several pages at
once? I fear that Father, when he sees this, will say, "this fan, even the
idea of it, would turn poor Nicola Tesla in his grave!"

The most welcome response at this moment would not be word
but deed: a brief absence followed by the slipping of a small vel-
vet-lined leather box into my suit pocket. But my sister is a woman
of words. My collaborator through all stages of my life, my champion and gentle, at times awkward critic, my sister's non sequiturs
occasionally betray a prescience. She pauses in reflection, as if to
absorb my proclamation, reclines herself on the Invalid Couch, citing date of patenting before doing so, of course, to earn the repose
(a gesture I take for granted, like a prayer before a meal in certain
households, until I notice Cecilia's bemusement), gazing blankly, as
is her habit, then begins: "A ring is a convention, Brother, indis-
putably." Then, at a volume unfortunately considerably greater
than that in which I delivered my proposition, a volume more
appropriate to a sermon, she continues, "but there is much to be
said against one." She goes on to say that she would not call me
guilty of inertia or irresponsibility or paucity of devotion for failing as yet to procure a ring but rather of inadvertent judiciousness.

Clearly, I was naive to assume the possibility of expedient exchange between my sister and myself. No question can elicit a cursory reply.

"Rings, casually displayed about the finger, possess many perils of which the average person is all too ignorant." All the while, she continues to manipulate the winch, raising and lowering the angle of her back and legs. "Firstly, it can easily catch on a railing or hitching block to terrible consequence."

"We have entered the age of the automobile, do not forget, Eleanor."

"Do not mention that cursed contraption," says Father, who has yet to reconcile with Mr. Ford over the many passengers who abandoned ship, if you will, jilting the rails to embrace the road.

"I need not cite particular examples, you may trust that they have been documented. In sum, is a ring worth the exchange of the finger it was intended to adorn?" My fiancée and I look at one another, she uncertain as to whether the rhetorical question should be answered. The pause, unfortunately, inspires my sister to continue. "There is so much to be mindful of when it comes to rings, to which we have all come to attach so much sentiment and significance. Should it not be a lesson to us that Mr. Keeler forty years ago divulged that Saturn's rings are composed entirely of tiny meteor particles, rather than the solid substance we had previously assumed." At this point the couch's latter segment is raised so high as to obscure her face, in fact, her entire person. "With modern thinking, rings can be revealed to be unnecessary, unreliable, one might go so far as to say . . . deceptive."

MARY CAPONEGRO

How can Cecilia interpret this as anything but disapproval of our engagement? (Always, Sister's digressions are permitted, never mine.) This evening—is it too obvious to state?—is not proceeding as I had intended. And it is far from over.

In the early days there was some flexibility in the evening's choreography. "All right children, take your places," my father would say, to move the program along. "What should we defend: molecular theory or photography? Logarithms or the kinetic theory of gases? The Laws of heredity or the telegraph? Trolley cars and the electricity they supplied to the dentist's office. Or balloons? Who are the relevant personages?"

I might then reply, "I shall be Montgolfier, Father, sailing through the air above a huge crowd gathered at Versaille below. Sister, meanwhile, shall take the role of Rittenhouse-Hopkins."

"What is the dispute? Say it, Thomas. What is at stake? What is the evidence?" And no matter what the chosen content, the exercise would invariably conclude with his censure: "Even when I let you pick from anything or anyone in history, you bungle it! All right, let's try again. What will it be? Cetrifugal pumps? Or the discovery of Neptune? And what is the difference between invention and discovery?"

But now that we are older, Father does not suggest, he demands. And it is even more difficult to make excuses; the stakes are higher— though this does not keep me from trying, particularly since I wish to distract Cecilia. "Father, you know that both your children have a fondness for the tangent. Sister knows a great deal about the planets from our preparations over the years. Perhaps there is a future for her there. You recall the many fields of study we investigated under your tutelage. It is noteworthy that the first female astronomy professor was appointed at Vassar in 1865, over half a century ago." I am rambling.

"Do then let me . . . note," (this last word he would inflect with disdainful emphasis even if he were not mocking my diction) "that the lady professor didn't make the discovery about Saturn, did she?"

"Well no, no indeed, but in time, one may assume, a woman may make such discoveries, don't you think, Cecilia?"

"In fact there are women inventors; one doesn't hear about them much," my fiancée supports me (as she struggles to support herself on the 1765 gondola-type Marquise, enveloped in its vast cushion, her shapely calves crossed, her hands in her lap).

"What is the difference between invention and discovery? Do we have to go over one of the first lessons I ever taught you?" He speaks as if Cecilia too were implicated, as if she by association now were responsible for all the learning we have failed to assimilate. Clearly Father is eager to return to the games, he has no interest in open-minded discussion. One would never know that a distant relative bearing our name was among those men proudly present at the first Women's Rights Convention in 1848, some eighty years ago.

"My point is this: with all her learning, Sister might profitably aspire to such a position. Women now take rightful place alongside men within the sciences as well as politics."

"Yes, think of Congresswoman Hattie Carraway of Arkansas, for example," Cecilia embellishes for me. "There were nine women, I believe, in the seventy-first Congress."

My sister, who ought for the sake of both her brother and her sex, be my ally, interjects from the Invalid Couch, "No, Brother, it is not healthy to gaze up at the planets. This can lead to losing one's head in the clouds, so to speak, and increase vulnerability to the beaks of passing or swooping birds, and more concretely, may I say, an eye avulsed by birds is not a pretty sight, though ultimately intriguing in its asymmetry."

Sometimes I think my sister's eyes stand forth so wide as to invite all things to fly into their ken, as if her face were a mask hung on the sky. She need not even tilt it upward. So far apart are her eyes, moreover, that her interlocutor is impelled to stand back, farther and farther, with the hope to bridge their distance by optical illusion, when they converge in the manner of railroad tracks.

Cecilia counters graciously, "But Miss Smalldridge, if I may add something, don't we traditionally look above for inspiration—look to the stars, so to speak? Your brother's aspirations are neatly suited to the metaphor, it seems to me." How courageous is my fiancée, treading among wolves—or griffins or ghosts. She thinks she is at a gathering among intellectuals such as occurs at her own residence, or at the settlement house, characterized by educated open-minded conversation.

But all "outside" perspectives bounce off Sister's at an oblique angle. Only an experienced listener can detect the degree to which her response integrates Cecilia's comment. To others it would seem as if she merely carries forth, oblivious to interlocution: ". . . although to gaze too assiduously at the ground one might garner equal injury falling upon a key in a door. This has also been documented—for keys as we know can lead to both grief and exultation."

Oh that I could find or craft a key like Penelope's of bronze and ivory, with which she searched for Ulysses' bow, to raid my sister's jewelcase or dresser or wherever her useless souvenir lies glittering, festering. I would try even with a second century Ptolemaic rake of iron or with Sycamore Wood from the Monastery of Epiphanius at Thebes (no matter how crude or ancient the tool, no matter how distant an ancestor, how atavistic to Yale's thin slip of steel, ornately garbed as it would be for this mythic occasion to purge my poor Eleanor of her past).

When we first investigated the realm of bolts and tumblers, I sought Mother's blessing, asking her to test me in Father's absence on the body of information. But a pursuit so ostensibly "open and shut" did not appeal to her.

"Keys," Mother would muse. "The truth is, Tommykins, I don't give a fig for a key unless it is cut from the alphabet in the service of music." (For her, to learn my ABCs included learning the alphabet's first quarter in a different, so-called universal, language: hence, my trained ear.) She bid me reflect on the sound of a dropped or raised bolt: the coarseness of its music in comparison to

MARY CAPONEGRO

harmonic transpositions. Why, she asked, would one choose to read the notches on a key's winged tip rather than the stacked sharps or flats whose signature moves from the threshold of one sonority and thus sensibility to another? (What, after all, was utility in the shadow of sublimity?) "Oh darling, don't be vexed. You know your mama is impractical; bank notes mean less to me than these notes on the staff! Keep to your tinkering if it pleases you. As for me, I'd rather play!" Then in response to my dejected look, "Here's a tip. Don't listen to my words, only my music," after which what Sister calls the siren's song commenced. (Is it not fitting that Berlioz, in his published memoirs, construed the harp as a siren?)

But between one harp's image and another is the face of my sister staring into a keyhole, peering, wincing, until her eyes hurt from squinting (compounded by the strain of her prodigious reading). "Nora, Nora, rest, please, I'll manage myself, it's my responsibility." But she would not leave her Tommy to do Papa's bidding, knowing full well my less adept intelligence needed her contribution (much as she might have preferred to be occupied full-time with her beloved references to aberrations).

Her squint would later seem to me the perfect metaphor for how a beholder would be obliged to regard her own peculiar— could one use the word *beauty?* Sister's face, indeed her entire aspect, seems arranged in the manner of a Gothic keyhole, which is only a slightly more emphatic indentation carved within an elaborate design, and lies hidden within a maze of activity and curve in a corner rather than at the center. Sometimes in my more vitriolic moments, I wonder, was that cad Cranshaw intrigued by a dissembling keyhole, and did he snatch it for its novelty alone? Did he seek to fashion himself a key by peering, clinically, into an aperture, only to meet with indignation and resistance? Did he deem eccentric Nora a parautoptic lock for which he anticipated no need for key or combination?

But Mama, see, your Tommy is a tumbler too! He can lock his body into place—falling, tumbling, somersaulting down without the least grace. You told us to think of the banister's spindles as a wooden harp. You told us that if it's true, our feet play scales each time we climb, up or down. So down the stairs I go, age five or six, taking her too literally, then having to lie a week on a mat in the parlor, stiff-necked and sore. But wasn't it worth it for the exhilaration of trying to make my whole body mimic her hand? Mama hadn't bargained for an entire trunk with neck, head, and legs dragged on the heels of the foot! Sdrucciolandi! Hear the glissing of the harpist's hand over strings replaced by the thud-ding of a boy's body against hard wooden steps. (Instead of an average child's olly-olly-in-free! or Geronimo!) SDRUCCIOLANDI!, I shouted again as I tumbled down. (But I would never confess my private aviation scheme, not even to Nora, who knew intu-itively—told Father, "simply slipped.")

"You clumsy kid," he scolded, unconcerned with whether legs or arms or neck had broken, "can't you do anything right?" But he might more accurately have asked, can't you do anything not in homage to her harp and her? And even then I would have known the answer: No! No! No! And no again, and furthermore,

MARY CAPONEGRO

how can you do otherwise? How can you not be my ally? How can you leave to me, a mere child, this overwhelming task of adoration? Try to teach me something someday that my heart can use! It would be unfair to say he isolated himself from me altogether, for in his way Father too sought fellowship, a filial camaraderie, but entrepreneurially, if you will, in the manner of the father/son inventor teams. To see Hubert and Thomas E. Smalldridge on the same list with the Yales, even the Cousineaus, the Nadermans (despite the inferior preoccupation of the latter two: harps) was his most fervent wish. Even Father is capable of the occasional concession, so desperately does he cling to the dream of my success—just as Mother wishes she could redirect her amorous history to find a composer/performer collaboration on the order of the Krumpholtzes or the Spohrs. But what Mother sought to gain through fantasy, Father sought through force.

Mother's ways were anything but crude or brutal, and this gentle grace was evident even in the most basic motion of a harpist's technique: a hand closing in upon itself as the thumb meets the other, longer fingers: simplest yet most evocative of gestures, as elegant, to me, as the silhouette of a crew of limber oarsmen stroking across a glass-smooth lake in perfect synchrony.

Father accuses me of being all thumbs at my inventing, but I have seen the thumb do astonishingly graceful things, particularly in relation to the strings bound by Mother's golden non-isosceles frame. Right-hand harmonics, for example: who would ever dream that the ugliest, chubbiest finger could persuade the harp string to yield the most delicate, ethereal of sounds—as if the string's own soul rose up above it calling, as if the string sprouted wings, and took flight. Or glisses, where the thumb spills downward, melding sound, timbres moving from full bodied to attenuated as the forefinger then reverses course, perhaps assisted by the middle finger to make parallel thirds. (My thumb, I swear, I'd make ingenious uses for it, should I ever have the privilege to peruse Cecilia's softest skin.)

The same index finger with which Mother executed ascending glisses would come gently forward to seal her—implying my—lips when I protested too much. Of course I'd hush, forgetting my complaint, to see the very finger that could produce such ethereal sound suggesting silence. Of course I would, I who stood speechless in the museum before the primitive eloquence of the gleaming, corpulent, bald-headed Cycladic figure, whose marble thumbs, despite the absence of actual strings, seemed ever-poised for strum or pluck.

Father, I would like to say, with your techniques I may indeed become all thumbs. On any average incendiary day, his surefire mnemonic method was to have me demonstrate the striking of a match and then recite, while holding it aflame, the history of how they came to be produced in books. Such provocation, he insisted, was the path to maximal efficiency. Accuracy and speed of information would avoid a burn. "Perhaps a cattle prod next time," I once told Nora, out of Father's hearing.

LET ME ASK THIS, LADIES AND GENTLEMEN: *When Edison created the phonograph, did he conceive of its potential for*

MARY CAPONEGRO

entertainment, for music? He did not; he had considered only the pedestrian functions of speech. When Yale conceived his thin slip of steel, did he realize its enormous potential for the door? He did not; he was preoccupied with inventing a means to secure drawers and cupboards.

Even the most illustrious inventor is imperfect; even the most gifted has his blindness, at least myopia, which often means he cannot see all implications of his very genius. For no one man can be as thorough as posterity.

And just how thorough could I, Thomas Edward Smalldridge, be, on that excruciating evening many years ago, when I was eight, and Nora thirteen, and we took turns peering at an inscrutable hole in a door, our eyesight weakened by lack of sleep? I am effecting a chord's resolution, I am completing a scale, I am retrieving the tonic, I am shaping a musical phrase: these things I imagine, to no purpose, as I tentatively, then desperately, tinker with tumblers, escutcheons, springs, and plugs, in my sweating hands, in the fading light. We have been in the room for hours, up to our ankles in metal dust, and our escape is solely, literally, in our hands; from a lathe and these assembled materials, and through trial and error, we must create the correct key for this locked door. Suddenly our month of research seems worthless. Father, away for days, has been even more zealous than usual, for Linus Senior and Junior Yale are the team he means to mimic, the father and son he yearns for us to be, and alas for the daughter as well as the son, he thinks he can force the issue.

Habits, as we know, die hard, and hands that tinkered all through childhood crave activity in maturity as well. What else might we do in our "adulthood" to exercise these fingers?—for of course we would feel idle with no project. We could, for instance, sit together on the S-shaped 1870 Confidante, and shuffle the deck of cards from the B&O Railroad (the back of each harboring the symbol of Illinois's state crop). This deck is the extent of amusement that Father allows in the house. Could I offer these to Cecilia as diversion, or allow her to play solitaire while we persist in our larger, far more alienating game? There is no room for eensy weensy spider in the parlor, not for a grown man.

LADIES AND GENTS, THE HARP CRIB

May I present the innovative Harp Crib—one of the most satisfying inventions of all time! One might say it kills two birds with one stone, but I prefer to modify the brutal idiom: feed two birds with one worm, for instance, sleep two birds in one nest, or best of all: soothe two birds with one song. It owes something to the famous Harp Bed, and in fact can be purchased in a set with that other noble furnishing. Particularly if the harp bed is in the service of a pregnancy, the harp crib is the ideal successor. For once the child is born and the mother regains her vigor, she can move from rest to child-tending without loss of musical activity. She need never be completely separate from it, and she can gently usher in her infant to the world of music-making. Nursery rhymes, for example, can be plucked on the spindled side of the crib, which is, I'm pleased to say, available in two or three octave range!

Eleanor is relentless in her resolve to correct misconceptions: "Even more suspect than the tradition of ring-bearing might be the institution of marriage that stands behind it. Perhaps we enter into it with too great haste, with insufficient scrutiny."

"Here, here," says Father, "I'll toast to that!"

"No, Father, toast instead to Captain Martin Van Buren Bates and Miss Anna Swan." Sister speaks as if they stood before us, having stepped that moment across the threshold. (Thank goodness they do not, for where would they sit?)

"Are they relatives?" Cecilia whispers.

"Oh no, strangers," I correct her. "Dead ones."

Eleanor carries on: "Be assured there was no ambiguity in the union which was cemented at St. Martin-in-the-Fields in London in 1871, marking these two renowned exhibitionists as the tallest married couple known to mankind. The sum of their collective height was fourteen feet and eight inches, more than half of this supplied by the female."

"She took the worn concept of a June bride and in every way elevated it, wouldn't you say, Sister?" (Cecilia rolls her eyes but squeezes my hand in affectionate acknowledgement of the poor pun.) Eleanor, meanwhile, ignores me or responds in her next comment, as usual it is difficult to interpret which: "The groom was clearly presidential in more than name only." Poor Cecilia, accustomed to better wit, must endure our peculiar Smalldridge humor.

"What could be more apparent than that these two individuals were destined for each other, and for all the world to see." All the world, thank heaven, is not present now to see my sister's bizarre beaming smile, or they would assume that she herself had been the officiate at this wedding. "Should not every marriage require distinction of this degree, distinction sufficient to be deemed patent-worthy?"

I fear my sister is expressing disapproval of my plans and that I am being punished with this public lecture for failing to confide to her my romance as it blossomed.

"In point of fact, poor judgment . . . or uncertainty"—even a passing glance from her appears dramatic—"makes itself known in many useful if awkward ways, Thomas, such as in the case of the young man who found himself stricken deaf and dumb when he asked the father of his intended for her hand. The body in its sudden and, happily temporary, muteness, signaled him to wait, not to act."

> *Admittedly, as with the Harp Headboard, the sweeping curve requires some adjustment on the part of the viewer. Of course, in bending to lift the infant from the crib, one must favor the lower side rather than the higher. Playing with the child need no longer be at the sacrifice of playing an instrument, for the reassuring gaze of the mother's face can be at all waking moments available to the infant. (When the infant sleeps, the mother has the option of returning, if fatigued, to the Harp Bed.)*

Oh Eleanor, I want to shout, to beg, don't you understand the greater absurdity and gravity of my plight: before I can ask Cecilia's father for her hand, I must beseech our father for what

MARY CAPONEGRO

should, in accordance with tradition, adorn that hand! (Besides, I have read the account; she has shown it to me before. Why does she omit the fact that the young man, once he is told yes, regains his hearing?)

As if she sensed my discomfort at this subject, Cecilia again rescues me: "Is it your theory, Miss Smalldridge, that all bodily afflictions may have other than organic cause?"

"Theories are not of much interest to me, Miss Crittenden, I leave theories to others, and for my part, there is nothing as fascinating, as instructive, as the organic. What had we been saying? Oh yes . . . sometimes causes of auditory impairment are the result of pins or carob nuts discovered to have fallen into the ear." And she begins to jab her head to the left toward the floor, hopping on one foot, as one does when trying to eliminate water from the ears. How can I stop her from embarrassing herself? Or is it my own "face" I would strive to save? (As if there were such hope at this point.)

"Do they sprout there, Sister, in the ear's canal, as do beans in the bowel?" I must sustain some levity for Cecilia's sake—good Lord, for my own. There was a time—I swear there was—when Sister and I had playful exchange. But now she does not smile, instead proceeds unhindered, thank heavens, having ceased to hop.

". . . and in the case of molten pewter poured by a wife into her husband's ear while he slept."

"I daresay that had not been a necessary, patent-worthy marriage in your estimation, Sister?" A wax cylinder plays in Sister's head, stuck, more often than not, in a single, slender groove.

"Have you heard of this incident in the history of medicine, Father?" (She turns from us, disgruntled. Perhaps I am too unrelenting in my interruptions.) "Such perfidy wives are capable of!"

"No question of that," Father replies, "but this, Nora, this was obviously an act of mercy. I'll bet that wife played some damn instrument or other, and he begged her to stop pummeling him with all those notes. She put him out of his misery! Take my word for it." Suddenly the prominence of Father's ears seems even more exaggerated—as if they had swelled, or angled themselves more severely, in response to the constant pressure of his conductor's cap (which Sister and I have agreed, serves to hide his receding hairline). Nor can one ignore the forest of his eyebrows, making a thick ridge the full length of his face, as if their proliferation might upstage the brim. The tiny brown beads beneath them might well be lost if they did not possess such a piercing quality. What's more, the unsavoriness of these features is compounded by his vulgar pantomime: index fingers wedged in ears while an unvoiced scream displays as much metal as any length of railroad track. I will not encourage his shenanigans by looking. I must defend Mother's honor even if futility is guaranteed.

"No, Father," I entreat, "don't compare Mother's music to pewter; if there be earthly analogy, I would propose a far more precious metal. Gold is surely what Mother spins in our midst, or better yet, gold mist!"

"Precious is the word all right, TomBoy, for your fancy metaphors. Eleanor, your brother thinks his mother is a fairy

MARY CAPONEGRO

princess. What do you think? Better get out the sweeper to clean up all this golden fairy dust! No, I've got it—melt it down in one big batch and pour it in my ears! So I wouldn't have to listen anymore. Me and Mr. Molten Pewter. Oh did I get it wrong, TomBoy? You look unhappy. If she's not a princess then I suppose she must be an angel, right? Just like that fancy harpist, Mrs. Crumbbun."

"Krumpholtz, Father."

"Right, Crum-holes . . . hey, isn't she the one who never got hers for driving her husband to suicide? Couldn't tarnish her glittering reputation because of her wings . . . I mean hands!"

"I think she is more likely a harpie, don't you, Father?" Eleanor asks. "Mother, I mean." Sister and Father chuckle in a most offensive manner. This is not the kind of levity I had in mind.

"Cecilia, do excuse their sense of humor. They indulge in the sort of private jokes that only families understand, those which seem to outsiders . . . justifiably . . . uncouth." In Cecilia's family far more edifying and courteous discourse is the rule.

"The body is indeed full of wonder, full of portent," Sister carries on. "We tend to single out mechanical inventions for admiration, while the body's innate creativity is ignored, or worse yet, shunned." No one has the power to stop Eleanor.

"Why, mysterious things indeed emanate from the body, things which can themselves merit the status of creature: the dermoid cyst, for example, unbidden extrusion of cerebral vesicle, eye, hair, molar tooth. In what category does it belong? The body's mascot? Neither conventional excresence nor an offspring, something far more wondrous; it makes us shudder. To bear a child is commonplace in comparison, wouldn't you agree, Miss Crittenden." (Cecilia's lips part but no sound emerges.)

"In my estimation, this is even more astonishing than the double scrotum, absent liver, anal tag, or flanged penis, although these are also hieratic scripts for our deciphering."

"What . . . what . . . truths might we obtain from them, Miss Smalldridge? My fiancée finally finds the strength to speak. "Could you enlighten us?" (Cecilia is just the kind of soldier my father wishes I could be, struggling to the death, against all odds, combatting squeamishness.) But I can see the slightest strain begin to reveal itself in her sumptuous roseate mouth—a slight loss of suppleness, in her tightening jaw, in the crease around her soft hazel eyes, as she frees herself from the plush incarceration of the Marquise and moves to the more austere Gothic bench, placed closer to the bathroom. I suspect that she has not, in all her dealings with the poor and underprivileged, encountered such a challenge to ideals or norms.

"Obviously anal tags suggest our continuity with other species, while the imperforate anus . . . tells . . . a story without end. Educational tools come in abundant guises, as we learn from the account of the boy who spent countless hours at the menagerie, examining every creature's feces. In this manner, he could identify each one. His time there was spent more fruitfully than an average child's, learning principles of induction and deduction less abstractly than a student of philosophy."

Desperate to divert the trend of conversation and perhaps to make expedient my punishment (although it is nowhere near the midnight hour), I rise and recklessly throw forth the design I have labored over since the previous wretched holiday that set this wretched year in motion: the Combination Teething Ring/Tuning Device. This cylindrical wooden T contains a brass sleeve bearing fitted to embrace each tuning peg of the most majestic of instruments. Its subtle genius is unlikely to be perceived, particularly given its scale—no bigger than a breadbox, no bigger, in fact, than a slice of bread, and ostensibly as pedestrian as the corkscrew it resembles (excepting the embellishment of a curve atop the T's shorter perpendicular line). A slight pause is the only hint that my gesture is acknowledged. Exhausted by this tiny gesture, I take refuge in one of the three seats of the s-shaped Confidante, my arm stretched across the armrest.

Then Father speaks. "Eleanor, your menagerie-boy makes a jim-dandy analogy for the patent lawyer your brother wants to meet."

I don't know where Father is leading but I do not like the looks of it, and thankfully Sister is likewise ignorant. "I beg your pardon, Father?"

"Well, don't you get it? If he looks at all of Tom's harpe-doodles—this hypothetical patent lawyer—he won't have to scratch his head too long before he figures out they're all produced by one inventor—since they're all . . ." He pauses to affect a concern with propriety, raising his shaggy eyebrows. "I'll let you fill in the blank, since we're in . . . mixed company."

Sister, to her credit, and to my consolation, is less inclined to encourage Father's antics when they are designed to ridicule me. Now it is she who changes the subject, or I should say seizes the subject in an attempt to render it respectable, discoursing on Rev. Henry Moule's 1860 earth closet and the mere two pounds of earth a day required to accomodate the average person's waste, much more economical than the water closet that outdistanced it in popularity.

Meanwhile, dear Cecilia sees how stricken I am by Father's comment, though surely I should be inured. She moves again to be near me, occupying the other curve of the Confidante's s, and places her arm over mine upon the arm-rest. She finds the strength to resurrect the lesser evil of my sister's previous train of thought. She eschews rudeness, but means, I think, to communicate to Father that his crude insult is not worthy of comment. (This silence is corroborated by Eleanor, whose loyalty is divided.)

"Is there a point you aim toward? I am curious as to the purpose of your argument, Miss Smalldridge."

"Indeed there is, and you will find it favorable," my sister announces, and as if to substantiate her claim, moves to the third and final remaining seat on the Confidante. "From the kitecycle to this . . . current . . . object . . ." (her euphemism, though benignly meant, causes me suddenly to feel as if I were naked before my bride and found inadequate, as if she were the one who said, with all apparent kindness, stand a little closer, hus-band, so I can see your wares—no, closer, closer . . . where . . . ?)

"the theme of Brother's inventions over the years is clear: ecomony, conflation, melding. In a word, marriage." Ah Eleanor, you do support me. (She understands the function implied by my device.) She too is appalled by Father's breach of etiquette and dignity, oblivious to her own. She will not stand to have me undermined before her eyes, and intends to proclaim to Father the health of my union with Cecilia. She is not against it after all. Yes, I sense she is about to lay the ring for which she has no longer use, before us, right next to my maligned invention, to honor the latter, to redeem it, and will pretend I have instead purchased the gift and appointed her my ring-bearer, and then will beam as convincingly as she did when she invoked the ghosts of Van Buren Bates and Swann.

But no.

No.

"How much it is to our credit that we do not indulge in the customary frivolous gossip of who has been and who is to be wed, and focus our attention on the more arresting unions that occur organically," she says instead.

"Do you mean recent experiments in the hybrid crops, Miss Smalldridge?" my indefatigable Cecilia inquires, "there's quite a future in them, they say. There is great potential in the collaboration of man and nature's kingdom." I should be grateful for her participation, but it begins to exhaust me, or is it the fact that she should be so supple and resourceful, while I sink deeper into lassitude and futility? I am consumed by wishing we might instead all be engaged in more conventional social intercourse. I would take comfort in such vapidity, in mindless parlor games, with the only crops in sight the corn insignia on the back of each playing card, as each woman coyly hoards her diamonds, aces, clubs, her spades, or hearts!

"I refer to other phenomena, not in the plant kingdom but our own human realm of physiology: for example, the young lady from Cleveland who possessed a double voice; many would gather to watch incredulous as she whistled through her throat without the slightest motion of her lips. In fact, nature had equipped her with a double epiglottis."

I must recover from my disappointment and participate. "This reminds me, Eleanor," I interrupt, "that Edison, for whom, as you know, Father named me, was accused of being a ventriloquist when the first reproduced sound was created. Young women in the audience fainted from the shock of hearing disembodied sound. In fact, Edison was startled himself. But soon we shall take sound in moving pictures for granted, just as we now take for granted the images that once seemed so fantastic. Do you remember, Cecilia, Eleanor, the panicked crowd's mass exodus from the theater to avoid the terrifying image of an oncoming train, as if the image could do damage, as if it had been real?"

I am answered only by my fiancée, who recalls reading or hearing of it.

"Those folks gave respect where it was due—the days before Ford, when the train ruled supreme," says Father. I imagine the train bursting through the screen, in hot pursuit, my father waving his cap out the window of the engine, "Gangway, choo-choo, Huey's coming through," like some drunken cow-boy, as all the well-dressed ladies and gentlemen, realizing their escape is futile, line the locomotive in supplication—prostrating themselves at its approach, only to be consumed. (What I will not reveal to him is that my current invention offers secret homage to his nemesis Ford's Model-T, discontinued after the fifteen millionth car.)

Nora's voice retrieves me. "The voice, Thomas, is only the first example. More noteworthy still, how does one reconcile a womb with two orifices, one of these with a connection to the stomach?" (What is the use to turn conversation in a more appropriate, edifying, universal direction?) "Our guest appears incredulous, but it was the only explanation for the seventeenth-century German woman who vomited her own fetus." (My fiancée looks about to faint.)

"Sister, truly, is it fitting to dwell in the grotesquerie of cen-turies past when so much progress has occurred in subsequent ones, even in the three decades that you and I have glimpsed?"

"Are we not cultivated? The more educated a person is, Thomas, the more he or she is able to appreciate the marvelous. You are my brother. And yet the bond of our blood does not pre-clude enormous differences in perspective. That is in itself a mar-vel, but I use it only as example. What demonstrates the mirroring of nature more concretely than a twin? And yet there are egre-gious deviations: one fetus delivered blighted while the other nor-mal, or more remarkably still, the blighted expelled in four or five or even seven months, while its healthy partner is carried to full term. Or the case of the double uterus, one in communication with the vagina and the other with the rectum. It is said that by the latter means, the mother chanced to become impregnated."

"Eleanor, I beg you."

"Are you not aware, Thomas, that some women menstruate through the avenue of defecation? How arbitrary, in the end, our habits come to seem. And then there are the pregnancies which nature never intended to sustain: the hermaphrodite whose breasts and dulcet voice were in no conflict with her beard and . . . standing organ. It should be no surprise that this account was presented by a Frenchman!" Even as she makes the disparaging comment, she shifts her posture, as if she could not bear to occupy the seat she chose due to its national origin (for furniture's evolution owes at least something to the French).

Before Eleanor has finished, Cecilia has fled the room, and I after her; Sister's relentless lecture never breaks stride, even as it competes with the unmistakable sound of retching. (No fetus is its fruit, however; the Lord does grant his modest favors.) Despite my alarm, I am ashamed to feel relief, mingled with concern, that my intended has not quit me altogether, has evacuated only the room (and stomach) but not the house. There is something perversely calming in my hunch that only such a visceral predicament would ever cause my Cecilia to turn her back to me. My shame is exacerbated by the disconcerting realization that even under these extreme circumstances, I find it hard to turn my ear from Sister. It is as if I were split in two, like a guest

MARY CAPONEGRO

between two conversations at a social gathering; but in lieu of pleasant if banal conversation, I am here sandwiched between harangue and eructation.

Like the voice of Edison's phonograph, just as ghostly, Eleanor persists. "Occasionally we find a fusion of the colon and rectum with the bladder, and no less frequently, coalition of the bowel with the bladder or urethra. Such conditions may be indeed inconvenient, a paradox of physiological economy. Duplex bladders are not uncommon, far more common, in fact, than a lack of bladder altogether." Her voice grows nearer with each sentence until she stands in the bathroom with us, a spectator to Cecilia's kneeling performance. "I am sure you are wondering whether each receives a ureter." (Dear God, does she aim to demonstrate somehow, as when she hopped to simulate the carob nuts inside the ear, how such a physiology would function? Why else would she be lifting her skirt? Does she mean to have the two of us urinate in tandem as an homage to the double bladder?)

"Wrong once again, Nora," I scold as civilly as possible, snatching her hand as if she were a child—"we wonder no such thing." But only deed, and not word, is daunted.

"The answer is yes. Furthermore, there was once even a triple bladder." (And all three, it seems to me, wherever they are, now burst, and rain their waters down on us, with the recklessness of pigeons.) I fear that I have already soiled Cecilia, made her reek of the stench of my own Smalldridge original sin—for it is not the family of man that bears this stain, but only this family into which it was my lot to be born.

"Cecilia, darling," I begin, with forced alacrity, "let me assist you in putting into context so much unfamiliar and . . . unsavory information. Eleanor, could you find me the page-turning fan so Cecilia can have a breeze?" It is the least she can do. The least is, however, too much to ask, for instead Sister invites the freezing January air through the bathroom window, none too warm to begin with, costs being what they are, and when I race to close it, she again assaults me with indecorous gestures, like some senile woman—thank goodness Cecilia is facing opposite—or a creature in estrus.

"I think I alone may have the background to understand the beauty of this esoteric opulence, through a metaphor fleshed out of music!" I bellow so that Father knows I remain a participant in the evening's games, and so that Cecilia's plight will not be audible to him.

"What is he talking about now?"—my father's unmistakable inflections.

"Indulge me but a moment."

"I guess she can afford to do that. I've been indulging him for twenty-five years!" Best to ignore Father, who allows me no such indulgence, as far as I can see, but feels free to indulge his own offensive habit of cigar smoking, suffocating us, and contributing, although she is too polite to say, to poor Cecilia's nausea.

I begin. "Dwell upon the following concept: twinned sound. Two for the price of one! An organ's—that is a bodily organ's—opulent excess is the equivalent of hearing, for example, on the harp, each note's resonance in duplicate! You see, Cecilia,

MARY CAPONEGRO

the instrument with which my upbringing gave me intimacy is in fact especially suited for this mirroring or twinning. Parish-Alvars, incidentally, is the virtuoso who made the most of this."

"Think of the wasted space in that boy's head—all those foreign names . . . What about respectable American men, real inventions, real contributions? I should have named him Parish! Parish-Alvars Smalldridge."

Ignoring Father's commentary from the other room, I explain that musical synonyms can be produced through the positioning of the pedals; that unisons thus sounded on separate strings create virtuosic and otherworldly effects. I urge her to listen to Mother's playing above us. The passage from Faure illustrates my point perfectly. "Listen to that chord," I tell her. Is it not the antithesis of the sound Cecilia's body now makes against her will? A harp, my love," I say, daring to stroke her lustrous chestnut hair as she purges herself anew, "alters tones each time the foot raises or depresses one of its pedals, unlike its relative, the piano, whose pedals have no function other than dampening or sustaining. The chord you just heard could not sound as mysterious on the piano, for $F\sharp/G\flat$ and $D\sharp/E\flat$ would take up two black keys and no more, whereas on the harp four strings multiply two notes: the G pedal, depressed, takes its string down a notch while the adjacent F pedal, raised, doubles the sonority." I take the liberty of sweeping her hair away from her face, out of harm's way, as she plucks from her bosom a scented linen handkerchief and holds it to her mouth, and I with my free hand run the faucet to provide additional aural camouflage. "And in fact prior to the double and even triple action harp, there was a harp with three rows of strings, called logically enough, the triple harp, in which each side acted as a set of sympathetic strings to the other, making abundant resonance"—the third and thankfully final purge punctuates my clause—"which I must confess" (I take advantage of our intimacy, transcending the stench, and lowering the volume of my voice), "dear Cecilia, presents itself to me as an apt metaphor for our bond." I take the further liberty of grasping the no-longer fragrant handkerchief in my own hands as a sign of further trust. In my peripheral vision I see Nora repeating her transgression at this most inopportune moment. Panicked, I drop the handkerchief. Cecilia unfortunately interprets this as repulsion, unaware I mean only to substitute for it the larger bolt of cloth that rides up Nora's thighs. All the while I manage to hold my beloved's hair; in fact, I pull it inadvertently, thus "doubling" the very discomfort which I had wished to alleviate. My dear Cecilia, if you only knew how much I wish to bury my face in the small square of fabric, because it comes from you, and all the more the place whence it came.

But to speak of intimacy in such a setting cannot fail to reassure a woman, even with Sister kneeling opposite—as if the bathroom were some bizarre church, each worshiper autonomous, addressing separate gods.

I hear Father shout, "Is this relevant?"

"As relevant as Eleanor's discourse, I should think." My courage to continue, is, I would like to think, due to Cecilia's presence, although it may be for a more pedestrian reason: the fact that Father cannot now hear me.

I carry on, raising my voice this time. "Thus Eleanor's mascots might be thought of as enharmonic organs: baroque bodies, if you will. Or consider a more concrete analogy: just the way some extravagant women might have two of a favorite garment so as keep one pristine: one for use, one for show (perhaps not the best metaphor, given these circumstances, I realize too late), these individuals of medical lore might be said to have a physiology in reserve, a beauty so rich, so conceptual, if you will, as to be beyond our present aesthetic."

I close with the fact that in London's Victoria and Albert Museum stands displayed a cross-strung chromatic harp with two necks, two crossed columns, and two double-strung bodies. (Again I lower the volume of my voice.) "I would love to take you there, Cecilia, and gaze with you upon the artifact that to me is pure romance, the instrument that embodies that which I perceive to be—if I may be so bold—our union of heart."

My voice is strained by the effort of having my arm wrenched behind me, playing an ongoing game of tug-of-war with Nora's garment—far less edifying than any version of "I packed my trunk." I must not dawdle. I gently take my beloved's arm and lead her back. Sister follows.

If only I were in complete control of the situation. At the very least—and perhaps no more—I have the power to sit Cecilia on the correct side of the 1835 English Back-to-Back Seat, with me beside her, and insist that she recline, leaning upon me. I can also insist that Nora sit on the other side, facing opposite.

Taking my fiancée's head in my lap, I recall that Mother often cradled mine on this same couch (while Father and Nora seemed miles away on the opposite side). These separations remain intact, it seems, for Father considers me out of bounds due to my discourse on the prime forbidden subject (harps), and Sister, having ceased at last her exhibitionism, makes certain that Cecilia's queasiness is not completely vanquished; she counteracts all romantic gestures (perhaps in reprisal for my thwarting her "performance," or perhaps to ensure our return to the Dolphin Toilet), by subjecting my fiancée to further verbiage concerning supernumerary mammae, a woman with two nipples on a single breast, a nipple on the face below the right ear, a man with three testicles in a single sac, etc. etc. etc. Her narration takes us straight back to the menagerie. (My poor misguided Cecilia thought at last she would find civilized common ground in botany when Sister began to speak of polyorchids, but Eleanor was referring to those flowers that bloom between a man's and woman's legs.)

But at last my sister journeys from anomalies in physiology to those man-made—shall I say, *this*-man-made?—coming full circle to the subject at hand. "Something as simple as this teething ring/tuning device is a cousin of the marvelous—that quality of which Thomas and I were recently speaking. It marries the needs of the mouth, the hand, and the peg of an instrument, with admirable humility. Consider the brilliance of the T-shape's simplicity: no more than head and trunk. Its head placates the child while the trunk—that is, the perpendicular bar . . .

MARY CAPONEGRO

fastens wherever needed to coax a flat string up by increments. I do not say it is the most original of endeavors. A mere tool, I do not claim its creativity rivals that of history's great unsung heroes and heroines, such as the woman who birthed her own child without an obstetrician, or the man who rolled a wheelbarrow all the way to California without once stopping, or the man who comminuted a calculus by introducing a chisel through his perineal fistula until it finally burst through and fell to the ground." (She pauses, absently nibbling along the edge of the fruit of my entire year.) "And it brings to mind the iron-jawed man and the woman who could hold a cannon—as it fired, mind you—in her teeth."

"You are right to mention them, Nora, the kind of people who belong at the carnival—that's just where Tom-E-son here might find work if he turns his nose up at the idea of the railroad" (then Father turns his vulgar face toward me), "or maybe you'd rather ride with the hobos. See how you like sleeping under a Hoover blanket!"

When one considers the 730 kilograms that constitute the total applied tension in a harp's strings, Sister's case of the woman with the cannon in her teeth seems less absurd—or the magnitude of the tension supplied by a crocodile's jaws, which she has specified but I have forgotten. And what, I wonder, if one could somehow quantify the collective tension in the room, or the cumulative tension in my sinews over the twenty-five years of my existence? Now that is a project I would endorse. But daydreaming is a luxury I can ill afford, for it is my responsibility to move the evening along; I must cultivate an iron jaw and grit my teeth through what is left, lest the cannon of this evening's contest explode in my mouth.

"Let us move from these esoteric aesthetics to matters more pragmatic," I proclaim with as much authority as I can muster. "It is all too obvious, Cecilia, that my sister is enamored of anatomy. I have long encouraged her to seek a specialized education, now available to her sex. We have all heard of Miss Elizabeth Blackwell, who earned the first medical degree ever to be conferred upon a woman."

"That is a fine suggestion, darling. There is, I believe, an entire medical school for women in London." (Even in her weariness she finds the energy to support me. Only I who know her well can detect a diminution of her vibrancy.)

"Yes, yours is an even better idea, to learn with all the solidarity of one's sex. I often think that Sister would prosper under these conditions."

"Doctors," says Eleanor, summarily, "are not to be trusted," proving that she who has elaborate skill in the excursive has also, when it suits her, the ability to terminate discussion abruptly. It was insensitive of me, I only now realize, although desperately well-meaning, to launch the topic in the first place.

I want nothing more than to protect Cecilia, I want to shield her from that which is in poor taste, and yet, what right have I, I suppose, to find fault with Sister's somatic computations—I who once having mastered 9 x 8 and 5 x 12, ignored Boolean algebra for the circle of fifths.

Eleanor remembers as well as I how Father, schooling me in shapes, made me practice the drawing of one geometrical figure after another: rhombus, rectangle, circle, square. In these I distinguished myself adequately. But when it came to triangles I was shamed over and over, until he tore up my drawings in disgust. "Three equal sides, Tombone," he hissed through his teeth, "make an equilateral triangle and two, an isosceles triangle, but any idiot knows each side is a straight line; there is no curved line, ever! You can't bend it! That's not allowed." Nor did he care for the lines—oddly enough, made straight with perfect ease— that stretched in even increments across the distorted geometric figure. Instead of angles A,B,C inside the triangle, I marked strings that stood for notes from A to G, in octaves, all the way across, the c marked red, f marked blue, for verisimilitude. (Am I not in some small ways my father's son?) And after this he began our present tradition, each year more exhaustive, of citing exact sequences of inventions in correspondence with patent numbers, and citing every day's invention in its proper date throughout the year. (When I was not quite old enough to understand, he told me, in broken voice, "See this bent side, Tomason, see this busted line? This is what your old man brings to bed at night, because if a man can't make his son into a man, how can he ever take his own manhood for granted?") How simple it should have been to do a third time what I twice had drawn, but in spite of myself, my pencil veered each time, lost its way despite the tiny distance between points. And the more I tried to master it, the more precipitous was its deviation. Sister was bored by retracing so many times; for she had succeeded from the first attempt—her page replete with perfect triangles of every kind. It pained her, she would tell me later, to observe my incompetence, so she doodled (on the verso) to distract herself. The strangest of diagrams did I observe there after these sessions: geometry gone awry into anatomical shapes of immense distortion, grotesque figures, pendulous, misshapen, asymmetrical, unsightly. Father's cryptic remark somehow collided in my imagination with these disturbing drawings, and I delivered myself all the more fully to my inventions as an alternative, and antidote, to a disquieting ambiguous vision.

My mind, says Father now, is too soft, as if my head were packed with cotton wool. Then finding this comparison insufficient he makes a further analogy: my mind an ancient Roman road in need of more flint between the curbstones, thus suitable only for pack animals, not sturdy enough for troops. My mind, in short, requires military preparation, such as my father claims to have had, if only briefly (a story whose details remain to us as shadowy as those regarding Sister's romance with Dr. Cranshaw) in some undisclosed conflict, perhaps the Spanish–American War. My lack of such experience is yet another causal thread to my inadequacy. Not having served our country in the most manly of ways, I thus could not bring discipline to bear upon my day-to-day endeavors. (For Father perceives a scholar as a soldier in the service of knowledge.)

We take for granted, LADIES AND GENTLEMEN, *the existence of the Player Piano, but what could be more exotic
than a Player Harp? Where would the pluckers be hidden,
you ask? And I propose to you that my sister fashion transparent prosthetic hands. Where would the harp rolls go, you
ask? And I say, ladies and gentlemen, that they curl around
the column and slither between each string, like paper snakes
weaving through the entire instrument. (We can consult
Puccini's* Turnadot *for precedent.)*

"What horror is he proposing now to toughen up my Thomas?"

How could I have missed her entrance, or noticed that the
Ravel had ended? She seems all the more statuesque when she
makes these grand appearances, and I can easily imagine the hush
over a crowd as she appeared on stage (attired in flowing garments
and luxurious coiffure) and floated toward the harp, or the curtain
parting to reveal her already in the embrace of her instrument.
(Whether she played in hell or heaven, her posture would be
impeccable, and how could any onlooker resist a second glance?)

It is fitting that the story of Orpheus and Eurydice was
adapted by Gluck and Handel for instrumentation that
includes the harp, for in my private musicology, I am Orpheus
reconstituted, unable not to turn and look back, despite the
dire consequences.

Most years Mother has missed the "festive" stroke of midnight; this year she is earlier, but alas, due to my recklessness, she
has not arrived in advance of the unveiling. "Darling, have you
impressed them yet?"

"Mother, you descend to us!"

"Don't worry, you didn't miss anything," says Father.

"Well, who do we have here, a guest? Really, Thomas, you are not subjecting such a lovely young woman to this tedium!"

"Have you come for Thomas's unveiling of his creation, Mrs. Smalldridge?" Cecilia is visibly relieved to meet a new member of the family; color returns to her lovely cheeks.

"As far as I'm concerned, my dear"—she is not nearly so tall as the fabled Miss Swann, but her neck suggests the grace of that elegant bird—"an invention is something in no more than two or three parts that was written by Bach!" She smiles, a smile both provocative and solicitous, and winks, then furnishing a newly opened eye so blue and wide you would dive in before you had a chance to think of drowning. "Do you know something?" she asks my fiancée. "When I bought Thomas a flute for his birthday and the following year a clarinet, he showed great promise even without formal lessons (as his strict father would not allow them). But after practicing he would disassemble them and use the parts as building blocks, or building-cylinders, I should say, for other things, extraordinary things."

"This does not surprise me in the least," says she who already deserves to be thought of as my better half. "I have told my parents what a genius Thomas is." (Father takes the cigar out of his mouth to affect a cough.)

"Of course, he could have been perfecting his embouchure instead, and then we could be playing a duet for you tonight."

"One cannot perfect all talents, I suppose," says Cecilia, with a glance at me so reassuring I could melt, "and the more gifts the harder to choose."

"Mother needs no accompaniment, in any case," I say, for the first time of the evening feeling my face redden from something other than shame, "her playing is magnificent all by itself."

"Yes, tell me," Cecilia asks, "is that what we have been charmed by? Bach? I could not give it the attention it merited with the . . . party . . . going on."

"Oh no, dear, a period much later, an altogether different sensibility: the French. Very recent music in fact."

"That is Mother's specialty," I interject.

"Have you ever been abroad, my dear? To France?" Father and Sister wink at each other.

"No, not yet, but at the settlement house, we have the privilege of being exposed to the marvelous new trends in painting as well as other cultural activities. The controversial architect Frank Lloyd Wright, for instance, lectured recently."

"Yes, privilege is the correct word, isn't it? (She is astute, Tommy.) I used to go often by steamer before I had the children, then occasionally, and now, of course . . . how could one? I studied music in Paris, at a conservatory. Has Thomas told you? Do you have any idea how many harp teachers there were in Paris at that time? Take a guess. (I'll give you a hint. In 1784, there were already 58!) Oh dear, I sound like Hubert, demanding figures."

"And that's the only fact she bothers to remember."

"In any case, it is hard to keep up my studies in such isolation."

Sister holds her left arm up at an angle and makes a sawing motion with her right to mimic a violin's playing, facing toward Father, who puts hand histrionically to forehead and nods, and rolls his eyes. Nora knows I will not respond, but discouraging them with any efficacy is beyond my capacity at this point.

"In those days my instrument was evolving in fascinating ways: Claude, late in his career, was asked to compose for the cross-strung harp by Lyon at Pleyel (you remember it, don't you, Thomas, the one you used to think was the most sensible design?), and then Erard commissioned Maurice for the same— he had just missed winning the Prix-de-Rome, you see, and needed to distract himself from the disappointment."

"She is referring to Debussy and Ravel, Cecilia; Mother was on a first name basis with both of them."

"Poor, poor Maurice," Father pouts, dabs his dry eyes.

The violin gesture again.

"Yes, Cecilia," I say, ignoring the disrespect, the piece my mother plays so beautifully, called *Introduction and Allegro pour Harpe* was composed in only three days en route to a yacht cruise! Perhaps Ravel felt desperately the need for efficiency, mourning the year at Rome's Villa Medici he had lost. And it contains some of the most spellbinding technical effects available on the instrument. Would that I could work so swiftly and impressively."

"You can say that again," Father cannot resist to add for my humiliation. "I can't get over these composer-fellows, can you, Nora? Tossing off a little ditty, then soaking up luxury, at their friends' expense. And your mother expects us to feel for them!

What a contrast to a true inventor's life! Look at that photo-graph, on the wall, Tom boy, the one of Edison after staying up for five straight days to complete the phonograph. Now that's application. That's dedication." (We gaze up dutifully, Sister's head and mine bowed as before a saint's image. But why does Thomas Alva's own head haunt me?—pasted on every cylinder that con-tains an inner cylinder—the very custom of depicting head alone, unnerving, as if by analogy his rolls beside Marie Antoinette and the late ruler of Elam.)

"Did he stroll lush French gardens for inspiration? Did he lick pâté off his fingers? Did Thomas Alva climb some marble stair-case to stare across the grand piazza when he felt like taking a break?" (To dramatize, Father adjusts the 1780 chair designed by Benjamin Franklin to convert itself into library steps and climbs in pantomime.) "Not a chance, not a chance! Our tried and true, red-blooded, American boy sat there at his humble Jersey desk and figured" (he descends, collapses the steps back into a seat, and sits in the now restored chair, chin in hand), "tinkered, figured some more. Am I right, Nora?"

"I imagine his wife's contribution was not negligible, nor his staff's," I offer in my sister's place.

"I see the details I care for interest no one in this house except Thomas," Mother spares me what would surely be a scolding for my insolence by dismissing Father's entire impas-sioned interruption. "But you, my dear, appear to be a cultured young lady."

"By all means, tell her everything," Sister says, mimicking Father's maneuvers with the analogous 1793 table, conjuring a ladder from its underbelly, stretching it above the table's height, and taking her turn at this makeshift podium, courtesy of Thomas Sheraton. "Tell her how when Michelen Kahn performed Ravel's *Introduction and Allegro* you simply had to go, even with Thomas still an infant—and the same for Henriette, and Madame Wumser Delacourte."

Hearing Sister's excoriating tone, Cecilia instinctively mediates, a courageous and resourceful peacemaker. "Would you do us the favor, Madame, of performing at our settlement house? It would be a great inspiration to the other ladies."

"Isn't she sweet?" Mother exclaims, taking Cecilia's chin in her hand and gazing intently at her with bold benevolence (as my sister's own chin droops, displaying the widow's peak from her statue-like stance, as if the two heads were suspended on a balance). "It's been years, I regret to admit, since I performed outside the home. Although I hope that after going to Salzedo's new harp colony this summer, I will be more supple again, more professional."

Father actually jumps up from the Convertible Chair in agitation. "And where might that be? No, let me guess, the south of France? A Greek island?"

"Fear not, Hubert. I know you'd hate to have me at such distance!" (She winks at me.) "The colony is not abroad at all. It is in Camden, Maine."

"Wait a minute now. This is the first I've heard about this!"

bellows Father, even more agitated now. "The most useful scheme you can come up with during this merciless depression is to spend a month lounging in a colony of those . . . those meretricious instruments."

"It's the biggest word he knows." She casts a condescending look at Father. "I'm flattered, Hugh." Then back to us— "Only bile has the power to send your father to the dictionary. He must have been rehearsing. He's building up his vocabulary from 'All aboard!'"

"Mock me all you want. The train won't transport you to Maine, Julia, or fetch you back. How will you pay to get all the way there? Then he turns to Eleanor. "She couldn't be sensible, practical, and go to Wisconsin. She couldn't find her fresh air and trees at Green Acres like the rest of Chicago's citizens. Or even plan a trip to New York City to see the Empire State Building now that it's finished, instead of pining for her Eiffel Tower. She couldn't choose one of hundreds of available stops on the railroad's hundreds of thousands of feet of trackwork! No, your mother must be different. She must indulge herself as flamboyantly as possible, at any price!"

"And would you have me spend the rest of my days in this swamp on stilts they call the Paris of America?" (Father seems genuinely taken aback by this insult, the incisiveness of which is enhanced by Mother's natural stage presence, and the protracted theatrical pause it engenders.)

Again Cecilia tries to restore decorum by asking Father whether he has visited abroad, but Mother answers for him: "He once spent the day in Leipzig, I believe, because it had the largest European train station. Now where were we, dear? It's a bit of a hostile environment down here, I'm afraid; he can't even behave for company. You see why I am eager to sequester myself. No doubt you expected a charming story about how we first met instead."

"Oh no, ma'am," says Cecilia demurely, "I . . . I expected no such . . ."

"Oh come now, darling. You are young, and a woman. All young women are romantics, aren't they? Or we wouldn't get ourselves into the messes we do" (another theatrical glance at father). "Even my daughter had a brief case of that female disease so common that no one ever bothered to list it in any of the peculiar textbooks she buries her head in to forget. That, how-ever, is a subject in itself. Well, you may not even be interested, and it may as well be ancient history, but there is one—the charming story, I mean. I don't know that I've ever told the whole of it. Would you care to hear it?"

This remark is obviously addressed to my fiancée and myself, since Mother knows as well as I that Father and Sister have no interest.

"Why not, then? Where to start? My ambitions, I suppose. I thought I would marry a conductor because I aspired to orchestral work. In my conservatory schooling I had digested so many stories of marriages between performers, or composers and performers, harp-makers and harpists, or such, and I felt my destiny was some variation of that pattern—someone in Europe,

I naturally assumed. But on a trip back to the states from France I met him," she gestures, "met Hubert, on a train. I was charmed by his ocarina. (Thomas, I've never seen your eyes so wide, yes he did play an ocarina, believe it or not, in those days.) Back then he was handsome too, in his own way, a man of 'striking appearance' is how one would have described him, and what's more, not yet hardened; he flirted with me, and I thought, how clever, to be courted by a train conductor instead. (I didn't realize he had a higher station with the railroad and was usually in charge of the conductors.) The whimsy of it appealed to me; I'm afraid my capriciousness bubbled up. Why couldn't I have been like other harpists, mating with their kind, like Krumpholtz, whose chosen one played even better than he—like an angel, it was said: an angel-wife who became an even more reliable interpreter of his compositions than Krumpholtz himself."

"... And who then jilted him and ran off to London with a young lover, causing poor Krumpholtz to drown himself in the Seine; don't forget that part of the story, Mother," Sister screams in a most unbecoming shrill tone that only Mother's presence can elicit from her. She grasps the ladder to steady herself.

"That's a rumor, dear. Eleanor has no feeling for romance anymore, I'm afraid. What were we saying? How much more sensible that would have been. Hubert's right in that—I am not strictly sensible! If I were, I wouldn't have been so susceptible when he serenaded me with show tunes. He claimed my Debussy needed to be supplemented with American popular song. 'May I introduce,' I remember him saying as he removed and proferred his cap, 'Irving Berlin, Stephen Foster, George and Ira Gershwin, and Cole Porter? A more boisterous crew than your French friends with their pretty, blurry wash of sound. What good is music that evaporates? How can you remember it? Who can whistle fog?'

"This man who would seem to have lost the ability and will to charm: I cannot begin to tell you how he charmed me then. My mood perhaps. My youth. My velleity. In his uniform and his mischievous grin, the wrinkles around his shiny little brown eyes, he made all the Frenchmen that had courted me seem affected, insincere, absurdly formal. 'Who can whistle fog?' I heard over and over in my head as I toured the Midwest, giggling to myself. And on my return trip, he genuflected before the reclining seat in the aisle. (He was less stout then.) He made up a charming story—that he had reserved for me the patented proposal seat, of which there was only one on each train. In Europe they had none, he said, because Americans were the *true* romantics (with their inventiveness and independence of spirit). He told me there was a telescoping footrest which would extend even further to make a kneeling platform. There was one on each train: the 'proposal suite' he called it. In fact it was no differently outfitted than the ones adjoining it, and thus his discomfort was evident, as was his transcendence of it. Uniform and all, he genuflected, and said, 'I've lived three decades, it's time I married. You are young and beautiful, you have the whole world in front of you. But maybe even an angel needs to settle down sometime.'

MARY CAPONEGRO

"It seemed so wise, that intuition, at the time: a man who'd bring me down to earth. I think of our romance in relation to the coming of mechanization; one quickly enough cannot remember what it felt like to do by hand what now a machine achieves, but in the inversion that is this marriage, if you will, one cannot remember that there was ease and naturalness, in what is now relentless strain and effort."

Mother's disclosure is, I know, mortifying to Father, and thought indulgent by Sister, but I cannot help but be moved by her attempt to confide in Cecilia. Nor can I help but hope that her trust might assuage the trauma of these last few grueling hours of spectatorship. In fact, her confiding to Cecilia a fuller account than even I had known proves her wish to embrace her fully, as my fiancée, my wife, as family.

The Father she describes to my fiancée is a phantom to me. And perhaps Mother's extraordinary, rich imagination gives him a past he did not ever possess, or perhaps it is possible to become a different person altogether over time in certain conditions. Certainly Sister's rapport with Father is something less severe, with a suggestion of tenderness, but even Eleanor would agree that as we grew, we knew nothing but remorseless pedagogy. Therefore I, with no defenses, fashioned my own fantasy to meet instruction head-on, conducting a private cosmic interrogation:

Entire centuries self-destructing in my imagination—the glory of both Greece and Rome lost in an incendiary grandeur, as well as that of the Sumerians, Phonecians, Egyptians, Babylonians.

Question: What is three parts gravel, one part mortar?

Answer: A salad dressing you can walk on—you can, that is, until it shakes asunder in young Tommy's troubled psyche.

Question: What then is a road?

Any Roman could answer: stone walls laid on their sides.

And I ask, why then could not the roads stand up again, lift off the ground to roam earth as celestial bodies, a Stonehenge in flight, and leave in their wake the debris of stone and bronze and iron age: pottery shards, bronze pumps, waterwheels, sails, arrows in orbit through bows, levers, wedges, pulleys and screws, aqueducts, all aflame around a shell of steel that itself surrounds a wrought-iron core, reheated until the whole thing ignites and the universe explodes—you lose the whole shebang, pal—booom, so much for your order, Father, try to rein it all in and it explodes in your face.

Tommy, what on earth . . . ?

No, that IS the earth, you didn't know? It's made of steel, round a wrought-iron core—or is it my father's heart? Or the expulsion of my bowels, in which, for all I know, I'd find beans sprouting?

But as far as I, Tommy Smalldridge, am concerned, if anything of Egypt's splendor survived intact, it would not be a phoenix rising from its ashes—as was the symbol of our Chicago in the wake of its great fire— but a three-stringed harp, forepillar amputated, majestic in its simplicity.

"Thanks for the trip down Memory lane, honey, but hey, let's not get all sentimental. We have business to conduct." Father is now leaning all the way back in the 1906 Barber Chair and activating

MARY CAPONEGRO

the Vibrassage Machine, for no apparent purpose, other than, I suspect, to appear unaffected by Mother's narrative.

"And what business might that be?"

"The unveiling. What else?"

"But Tommy has presented his . . . invention . . . already." Though Nora makes the comment, he glares at me in response, first lowering the footrest and restoring himself to erect sitting posture.

"No, that can't be all you brought to represent a year of work. Not even you would try to get away with that. You're always asking me to indulge you, so this time you get your wish. We have a guest to entertain, after all." (I do not care for the sneer directed at Cecilia.)

"But it isn't midnight yet, Father?"

"No, it isn't midnight yet, but your mother is here and this is the quickest way to get rid of her. Tom still hasn't figured out that she comes down late each year on purpose. Her highness doesn't care to be bored. Though as far as I'm concerned, whether she twiddles her thumbs down here or between the golden strings behind her 'boudoir' door makes no difference."

"But Father," I say, ashamed of how tentative my statement sounds, "it has already been presented."

"Tom-Tom, your jokes are always feeble, but that's the feeblest of all. Don't dare make light of something so serious as the presentation, especially this year's presentation, in honor of the man I named you for."

I cannot possibly explain that my invention's modified T-shape is precisely in Edison's honor, to evoke the way the first letter of his name is scripted on his record packaging. (The relation to Henry Ford's Model-T was in fact secondary.)

"I'll give you a little more time to come to your senses, while we focus on . . . Fuller. Thomas will tell us what can be learned from Fuller." (This is a kind of cleansing the palate between courses, as it were—the part of the evening games when we are furnished with an exercise involving a single inventor of Father's choosing, as cursory or as thorough as he decrees, a rapid overview or the listing and defending of all inventions, complete with diagrams drawn on the spot.)

"What invention was created to house the thing you never generate?"

"You would be referring to the cash register, Father, in the vicinity of patent #420,554 and #420,555, with the price visible to the customer, then to both clerk and customer, and thereafter sporting a stream of other technical improvements."

"This, Son, is a progression of ideas; these modifications constitute improvements, pragmatic improvements that are socially useful. Now let's get technical."

"Very well, then, Father. The secret was a reversing mechanism: two sets of indicating wheels, front and rear mounted and connected together, so numbers read, in each case, front and back, from left to right and right side up. Thus, by 1891, both customer and clerk could simultaneously see the total of the purchased goods."

"And compare this to your own creations." (I am expected to debase myself, articulate the uselessness of my creations.)

MARY CAPONEGRO

"Here, I'll do it for you." (Just as well.) "Your harp inventions, boy, are not exactly 'visible to the customer,' are they? What they add up to is visible only to you!—a one-way street. See, your pop can make metaphors too, but mine make sense, whereas yours add up only in your dreamworld."

"Think of Fuller's Time-Punch Clock, etc." (I draw feverishly in case I am asked to supply a diagram.) "This invention should be in your head morning, noon, and night, as a corrective. What you need to know is that if we measured on it the hours you've spent in actual work versus whimsical work, it would record a FAT GOOSE EGG! Right this second, Fuller is probably inventing something else to make our lives easier. What are you doing? Mooning over the young woman, moaning about your money troubles—instead of putting on your thinking cap to solve both problems in one fell swoop. Think of Fuller, for Chrissake." (I have been all this while, what option is there but to think of Fuller?) "His broken hip made him become twice as industrious. He thrived on adversity! But you'll never create anything as useful as a railroad ticket machine."

LADIES AND GENTLEMEN, THE HARP BED—*not to be confused with its predecessor, the Harp Headboard, a far simpler invention. The difference is this: here the strings of the harp are coiled in an elaborate fashion to make the foundation of a mattress. The recumbent party must adopt a fetal position given the narrowness of the triangular base. Before the harp is gently eased upon its side to become a mattress, its winged compartments are detached to become closets; its*

gold crown atop the forepillar is hollowed to allow for
plumbing. Stored towels and sheets coil themselves like
springs until they are pulled out the top.

"Listen here, Tombone." I've been listening all my life—all ears, like one of Sister's prized anomalies; I may as well be literally, grotesquely so. "Do you want this as your legacy—this tripe? Is this what you want to be remembered for?" My body one enormous auricle: no speech, sight, taste, or smell, only a multifaceted receptacle for exhortation, censure, invective. "Better to be forgotten, anonymous, than have the Smalldrige name attached to this. It's bad enough that men devote their entire lives to making, making, making—maybe hundreds of inventions, and are usually remembered for a single thing. Our job is to remember that everything these fine men made took society one notch further toward perfection. But everything you make, Tombone, repeats your first mistake. No matter how many sham improvements you propose each year, I don't smell profit in a single scheme of yours. And I don't smell a shred of common sense."

(How could you smell anything, I want to ask, beyond the effluvia of the long brown cylinder inside your mouth. Rediscover, Father, the world outside the cloud of your cigar. Adapting your own pathetic courting line, I'd love to shout out, WHO CAN SMELL THROUGH FOG? WHO CAN SMELL THROUGH FOG? But I am too craven.)

MARY CAPONEGRO

Mother wanted to call my sister Eloise; she felt it would give a girl a Frenchish elegance, but Father, who nearly named her Alva—which would have linked us even more concretely—insisted on Eleanor as a compromise, allowing Mother to keep one syllable, surrender two. Hence her nickname Nora, which both my parents claim was my creation when I couldn't get the whole of her name out of my toddler's mouth; ironically enough the "EL" that was their bond evaporated in that "settlement." Had Mother had her wish, and had I abbreviated it in the same toddler style, then Sister would perhaps be nicknamed Wheeze? Here, Wheeze, dear Wheeze, . . . and how apposite considering Eleanor's fascination with a thousand maladies, and that we both have spent our upbringings in a cloud of smoke that chokes us . . . I may as well stand beside the train and inhale its fumes, I may as well take permanent occupancy in Edison's blazing baggage car and breathe that fatal smoke. . . .

And what if the trunk we children packed were indeed capacious enough to house all the world's progress in one alphabetical unfolding, and this fantastic trunk had been in the special secret corner of the baggage car on the Port Huron–Detroit line train, which exploded because Edison was so driven—or unscrupulous—or rambunctious—as to perform his chemical experiments on the job!?

I packed my trunk and in it I put the butcher, the baker, the candlestick-maker, did I say two *b*'s make an *a?* Why not make it three, go BOOM! Woops, let's start over: *a* is for Armour, *h* is for

Hammond, throw in Pullman, quick, add Swift and swiftly light the candlestick to create a conflagration more dramatic than Chicago's legendary fire—and please do not let even one invention, phoenix-like, rise again, let them all be reduced to ash, so that dust they shall remain.

But Father would not be amused, TANGENTS TANGENTS, he would cry, and not invoke the mathematical kind. Father threatens every day to put me to work on the railroad—even now when his threat is empty, for what job might I find when so few are available? He hasn't one himself. But this does not seem a factor in his rage. I am required in principle to follow in his footsteps by direct vocational emulation if I do not, through my own means, "make something of myself" at last—if I do not, in fact, outdistance Edison by next New Year. Each year this has been the threat, as jobs dwindled to nil. But still his threat has force.

"But Father," I protest, "Mr. Edison had in the neighborhood of 1180 patents . . ."

"Halt right there," he says, his palm before my face, as if I were some speeding iron freight instead of this tall yet slight, in fact, hunch-shouldered, bespectacled, unthreatening young man—his own innocuous son. "A boy who rounds off numbers, a boy who uses vague terms like 'in the vicinity of' will never have the precision to number every lever, every mechanism on a patent blueprint, such as every lever of Fuller's cash register . . ."

"As I was saying, Father, I can't even amass sufficient moneys for a patent application."

MARY CAPONEGRO

"It was not Fuller's first or only, Thomas, was it? If you don't put all your eggs in one basket, it's not a tragedy to lose the blasted basket, is it? If you would prove yourself," he says, "with even one worthwhile proposal, you'd have your application, you'd have a thousand applications, maybe eleven hundred eighty times a hundred! Can't you see, boy, I want to save you!"

I who have been all my life all ears apparently cannot see Father as my knight, my Christ, my nurse; I'd sooner remain blind.

"Fifty percent of inventions never pass muster at the patent office. Do you know that? I want to beef you up to withstand the pressures of the competition. I want to spare you the struggle for success."

I suppress the unprecedented impulse to place my hand on his shoulder. "Father," I say, "contrary to what you suppose, I do not wish to tax you into perpetuity. I must come to terms with the fact that my inventions will not likely ever please you. But I have another plan you may find more palatable."

All eyes are on me. "If I may be perfectly blunt, might I borrow money for a ring instead?" Silence. Dead silence. What I prayed might be transacted privately must be public instead. There was no alternative. I have risked all now. (Any other woman would be humiliated, but I know my Cecilia understands extreme conditions call for extreme measures.)

"I am certain you will find this a more practical request." This last statement I squeak out in no more than a whisper, in spite of myself, awaiting judgment. And judgment comes.

"Only a sentimental fool would marry in the height of

depression. Do you think poverty is romantic, Tomboy? Like failing? Your mind should be on essentials. Marry when you can provide for a wife, use your head, block that it is"—he cuffs me to reinforce his injunction—"if you still have one! He's about as sensible as his mother, Nora."

With all the temerity I can muster, having gone this far already in my insolence, I counter, "My mind is precisely on essentials, Father," taking my Cecilia's hand in mine, "though not material essentials."

"Ah, such piety, I could puke." I see Cecilia's barely veiled disdain.

"Perhaps my wife can provide for me" (soft but audible). Father looks disgusted. If I could hear his mind, I'm certain it would play the refrain of my childhood: if a man can't make his son into a man, how can he take his own manhood for granted?

"Don't I recall reading in the *Saturday Evening Post* that Edison made money not as an inventor but as a manufacturer?" my fiancée asks. The subtlest squeeze of her hand. (Is there a woman on earth more possessed of poise? Well, perhaps one only.) "How unconscionable that inventing, of itself, is not lucrative." (But even my Cecilia's diplomacy cannot alter the course of family history.)

"You make some money, Son, I'll match it," Father says, "but until then, I can't endorse your ruin. Where would you be as a laughingstock of Washington?—the young fool who dared to submit the series of trifles known as the Harp Series, when he should have been expanding mankind's contributions to transportation, communication, medicine, defense . . ." For a moment my every ear seals up against the unstanched flow of invective. "Now then, Thomas. Tell us all. How do you intend to 'earn' the new year?"

Sister rises and holds the teething ring/tuning implement up to his face as if it were a newly discovered archeological artifact of undeniable significance—the tibia of a Cro-Magnon man (unfortunately encouraging his jejune antics, for Father sticks out his tongue, pants, and barks). "Oh but Father, is it not a thrill to have combined these two very different functions!" she cries, with not just dutiful support but genuine enthusiasm. "On the one hand to soothe the gums that yield to dentition, inevitably reminding us of Yale's momentous inversion of the key's teeth, and on the other to boost the note to stand as erect as its neighbors, and what's more, in its precise relation to the notes before and after it."

"Tuning peg/teething ring my ass, son! Why can't you tune it with your goddam fingers?"

"But I do wonder, Tommy, how is it kept clean? And what about splinters?" Nora mutters to herself, scrutinizing it.

Now I stand up as well, dwarfing my creation. (The perspective is unfortunate. For one irrevocable second, I see how in Father's eyes, the thing could not be other than inconsequential.) "Perhaps I can explain more technically, Father—you see, only when the string has gone lax need the infant's teething be interrupted. And thus he can feel a part of the instrument's maintenance, sharing in his mother's whole existence. He is not

threatened or bereft, because he is continuous with his mother's instrument."

"Yeah, Tom-Tom, a highly technical explanation. That
clears up everything. Why, for Pete's sake, can't he make another
Kitecycle? You tease and tease and tease—just like your mother.
I should have named you Teasing Tom!"

> THE HARP-HAMMOCK
> *The Harp-Hammock is admittedly a tad cumbersome as it*
> *is, technically, a dual-harp invention, feasible only for house-*
> *holds in possession of two harps, each serving as a pole or*
> *surrogate tree from which to string the hammock. The ham-*
> *mock itself is stored inside the forepillar; the crown functions*
> *in the manner of a pot lid; it is removed and then replaced,*
> *after the cloth and netting are retrieved. Thus, unlike the*
> *Bicycle-Hammock, the Harp-Hammock does not precisely*
> *collapse. Rather, it gives ballast, with its twin, to the cloth*
> *support. (The inventor wishes it known that this compro-*
> *mise was not his first choice, for he has experimented, for a*
> *full year, with ways to actually collapse the instrument into*
> *a hammock, or ways to incorporate the instrument's tremen-*
> *dous weight into the design: lying flat as in the case of the*
> *Harp-Bed, to serve as a kind of suspended mattress. But*
> *many strong men would be required to fasten the weighty*
> *harp between two hefty trees, and the spontaneous nap*
> *would become a chore indeed.)*

"That juvenile contraption had so much potential—and young
lady, you'd better believe I tried my damndest to cultivate it. Lousy

MARY CAPONEGRO

Kitecycle. Has he told you about it?" (But of course I have told the woman I love about the one glimmer of hope in the underworld of my upbringing.) But Father's question appears to be rhetorical. Cecilia parts her lips to no purpose. "I'm sure he mentioned it while he sweet-talked you into being his girl. Hoodwinked you just like it did me. Did you kiss him for his pretty boyhood memory? Don't bother blushing; here's the more important question. Did he tell you how he conned us with its promise—the form that sailed in the wind as it was propelled by the pedals below—and how I struggled to help him build an inventor's empire of it? And for what? For what? To stunt his growth instead? To give *my* name, and worse yet, Edison's, to an imposter inventor!"

Father, more venomous than usual, is purple with rage, Cecilia pink with shame, and I, white with fear that this circus now consists of many more than three rings, and each one out of hand. My love is not accustomed to such dismissive treatment; she expects the same respect she accords others, but she has indeed come to the wrong house.

"Do you love his useless flowery language, Miss? Of course you do, it's fine for girls. His mother saw to that. Well, here's some poetry for you, since you all think I'm just a crude has-been conductor who can't cough up a rhyme: Tommy Smalldrige, who is he? A wine that won't age, a flower that won't bloom, an infant that soils himself well past the toddler stage, despite the most thorough training any kid could ask for . . ."

"Father, please, I beg you."

"Enough, Hubert." Ah, my guardian angel: she in whose

honor the teething ring/tuning implement and all its predecessors were made. This latest invention's shape is not only functional but symbolic, for it puts, not words, but a letter in her
mouth, as it were, allowing her to express her own sentiments
toward Chicago through Father's sensibility, with a crudity she
would never stoop to other than elliptically. You see, the *t,* were
it placed in the windy city's middle, three letters in, before the
second *c,* would rechristen it appropriately. (While for myself, the
same letter derives from Ford's Model-T, and its stem stands as
erect as might a finger leaping from the middle of a fist, making
an additional gesture of covert vulgarity.)

"Oh they're ganging up on me, they're going to stifle me."
Father play-acts trembling, embracing himself with his coarse
hands, one finger mauled in a fashion we were led to believe was
related to wartime valor, but I begin to suspect was the result of
a far less glamorous train accident—of being wedged between
two cars in carelessness perhaps, or of being in the wrong place at
the wrong time, happening upon a chemical explosion in a baggage car? He extends his arms with palms forward again in mock
protection. "I guess that's what it takes to get my wife to speak to
me directly. One command worth a thousand gossamer notes. It
sends shivers down my spine the way that twaddle she plays never
does. Why couldn't he have inherited at least my industry, instead
of this blasted whimsy? Who did that come from, Daughter?"

"Surely from his mother, Father."

"Yes, exactly. Thank you. Only one member of this household can be relied upon to give accurate answers. As to you" (he

turns to me), "from the time you were born, I called to you, Thomas Eddy, Son, so you might follow in the footsteps of the greatest of American inventors—let us have a moment of silence for our recently deceased Thomas Alva." Father bows his head. We obediently do likewise. "Do you realize this year's games are the most important of all, because this is the year that could designate you Edison's successor? And this is the year that you, more obstinate than ever, bring your sweetheart to tea! It's obvious the ambition in that name just didn't stick. It doesn't fit you. I should just hand down my watch and my cap and be done with it, so you'd at least have a respectable profession, and put an end to this waste and false hope."

I would not care to wear that cap and allow its oils to penetrate my scalp. For twenty or more years it has been removed only in exchange for a pillow during sleep—he who was allowed to sleep while his children continued to toil, allegedly for their own good. (I recall my shock when seeing him without it, and, seeing him, what's more, at rest—more startling than discovering a parent naked.)

"But how can one assess hope, Father? I implore you to recall the Paris Exhibition of 1881 and the critic there who insisted that the electric lightbulb would never be seen again. Please Father, do not assign me to trains." Why not beg? What greater humiliation can occur than has already? "Worse than a blown-up baggage car would be the interior explosion in a young man whose heart and soul is elsewhere than his work."

"Ex-plo-sion." He draws out every syllable as if the word were incomprehensible. An exploded . . . soul." Then he throws back his balding head so heartily as to unseat the cap and laughs. "You sentimental idiot! Are you sure some sissy Frenchman didn't sire this fool?"

"Not some *sissy* Frenchman, no," says Mother, goading.

"If you consider the vocations of the great inventors, Father," I interpose, "you will see a host of incongruities."

"Give me that in plain English, could you, Tom?" He stoops to retrieve his signature sartorial article.

"Very well, I'll itemize. Eli Whitney, for instance, had a violin repair business."

"You said that before."

"Yale was a portrait painter."

"And did that interfere, Thomas, with his great gifts to us?"

"My point exactly, Father. And Edison, as you know, was a man with very little formal education."

"Right again, that's why I educated you at home, for all the good it's done me. (Our Tommy is no John Stuart Mill, is he, Nora?)"

(I will simply carry on.) "Morse was a painter as well as a teacher of painting—the head, in fact, of the National Design Association."

"Tough life."

"In some respects it was indeed. You see, Father, his passion was historical paintings, but he was denied an important commission because of Fenimore Cooper's critical letter, mistakenly attributed to Morse himself. He studied art in Paris."

"And that automatically crosses him off my list! But let's

look at the other side of the coin too, while we're at it. Mr. Manuel García—a music teacher, remember?—who did something useful and invented that laryngoscope! It's my job, Tom, to see that you do something useful too, so for a dollar a week or fifty cents you'll do what duties you're assigned. And you could do much worse, Son, than be confined to the railroad; its progress is a mighty chapter in the history of invention. Maybe you need some review. Let's begin at the beginning."

My father says the French, for all their fancy phonemes and their linguistic pride, could not describe simplicity; it stumped them, in his words. Pullman Car style was the best they could do when they saw a train interior, American style, at the Philadelphia Centennial Exposition of 1876.

In France, you see, luxury was for the upper class, but the democratic Americans felt that any traveler deserves to sit in comfort. Thus the reclining chair found its way to the rails; what had been for barbers, dentists, and invalids an ingenious innovation became adapted for general use. (Now a shave and a haircut, or a cavity, or an illness weren't the only justifications to make your chair tilt back; you could simply be a traveler, specifically a railroad passenger.) But why should I give him the satisfaction of the information?—as he would insist upon a far drier delivery.

"Oh never mind. I couldn't stand the sight of you inside my train. You'd sit there useless and nervous, your legs crossed and your prissy hands twitching. Or you'd lie looking up at the ceiling, whistling some tinselly French tune to calm yourself down. Without even trying, you'd make a mockery of everything invented by the sweat of Pullman's brow. No, Son, where you belong is in the baggage car with the bums or clinging to the underside like a fungus."

Ah, Pullman, Armor, Swift: my father's Father, Son, and Holy Ghost! If I too blessed myself in the name of your entrepreneurial trinity, and made obeisance to you, would I stand more chance of success?

"Saint Pullman, Father, I believe, is the same man" (I interject with a temerity that surprises me) "who prospered off the patents of his competitor, Woodruff, and eventually drove him to ruin." At a volume that obliterates a lovely passage of Debussy's *Danse Profane*—I had not enough noticed her retreat, so caught up was I in Father's rage—Father retorts, "At least he had the drive to prosper. He didn't lollygag about. Greed may be a vice, but everyone in my uncultured circle thinks industry is a virtue."

What circle he might be referring to I can't imagine; there are no social gatherings, except this annual travesty, at our house.

"In this bleak time more than any!" he continues. "Even a mollycoddled boy who wants to stay a mollycoddled man should be able to see that. How many lazy greedy men, I ask you, have filled the pages of American history?" (Then he takes the pointer we refer to privately as his riding crop, galloping—as well as a thick-waisted man can—around the parlor from wall to wall, from head to head, nearly shattering the glass of the photo's frame. "Now this is an inventor, Thomas." He smacks Marconi on

MARY CAPONEGRO

the ear and delivers the Wright brothers a double blow—I suppose it's to ensure they not get off scott-free after beating out poor Langley for the patent. He whacks Ford on the nose—I suspect he always wanted to do that. I want to caress the stricken places and tell them, don't be offended, his striking you is only to make a point, he actually respects you enormously, a respect I covet greatly.

"And would you be so good as to tell me why, with your sister's help if you have to. What has this man done to earn part of my wall?" Before I can answer he strikes at another portrait and another. "You have only one thing you are supposed to do, and you can't even manage that! These men, the ones who should be your inspiration, labored in the working world and then toiled into the wee hours at projects no one else had dreamed of. These men . . ." (panting now, out of breath) "did not indulge themselves. They furthered civilization." And indeed, this frenzied ogre with a pointer seems a curious spokesman for a "furthered" civilization.

"Had you emulated Thomas Alva," Father moans, "you might have averted the crash of '29."

Why, I want to ask, is T.E.'s mischief valorous, while my earnest efforts alternately blasphemous or ludicrous? I should find my own baggage car to blow up! Next thing you know, he'll suggest I am the cause, retroactively, of The Great War. Or of another not yet taken place. "Surely, Father you don't imply . . ."

"He fixed at least one crisis on Wall Street. And each triumph of ingenuity led to a new job."

"Or a complication, such as a betrayal, Father. Edison's life was not a straight path to success."

"For you, Son, each flop is further from any job at all. Thomas Alva had no protégé. This is why we're in this mess, the country gone to hell in a handbasket. It was the crash that killed him, I swear it."

"More likely his relentless toil, his punishing schedule . . ." (I gesture, lacking pointer, toward the famous photo of his weary head after five nights of toil.) "Or simply his age. The man was eighty-three, after all."

"Why do you call it punishing? It had rewards. Because it consisted of more than simply dreaming? Mr. Edison wasn't afraid to apply his imagination in the real world: the world of men! Thomas Alva didn't shrink from places where risk is taken with real stakes—whether selling vegetables or newspapers or being resourceful enough to fix something so useful to Wall Street that they paid him a fortune . . . instead of some fanciful realm where one cockamamy invention is as good as another because they're all useless, frivolous . . . what more could I possibly provide you to give ideal conditions for creation?"

"Well, Father, if you object to the loan of a sum toward a patent application, perhaps what many specialists would deem the prerequisite of inspired thinking might qualify as more worthy."

"You mean a brain, Tom boy?"

I will ignore him, carry on. "That to which I have previously alluded: a gem to adorn the finger of the hand I seek to take in marriage."

MARY CAPONEGRO

"Well, well, well."

Here is my chance to elaborate—as eloquently as possible: "Just as lack of capital stands at the head of the minus column, if you will, Father, companionship has been cited by many inventors in a very recent study as a necessary condition for inspiration. The vast majority of successful inventors have become so with the moral support of their wives."

"How was that recent study conducted, may I ask? By going door to door, like our intruder? . . . beg pardon, I mean guest!—the young lady who gives to the poor by bothering the rest of us who have no money left to give." Cecilia's hand clasps her mouth. She is aghast. "And no prospects of replenishing it through our offspring's efforts! No one asked me about my moral support." Will Cecilia endure beyond this interminable evening, and if so, am I but one more exercise in charity—our destinies linked through my status as the culmination of a long career of nurturing stray dogs and cats? How could anyone abide this loathsome spectacle for any other motive? What has led me to this desperate measure?

"Or perhaps, Sir, you think wives are not capable of providing moral support. Perhaps you would concur with Mr. Mussolini that a woman's function is to be life's agreeable parenthesis."

He ignores her confrontation, addressing only me. "Do you think I didn't hear you the first time? I told you no. Is that the most inventive method you can conjure up—to repeat until no one can stand it anymore? Just like with your pathetic inventions—saying the same thing over and over disguised as something new?"

"Perhaps a ring of finely twined bamboo fibers," Sister interjects, dreamily, "such as those that Edison received at Menlo Park, New Jersey, would be unlike that of any other couple—a band that would glow in the dark, proclaiming the luminous nature of the union: a patented wedding ring."

I feel her hands placed protectively on my slumped shoulders, "Consider how the harp pressed against her belly when he was forming in it? Worse still, against her breast as she was feeding him, no doubt crimping the milk's flow, obstructing his nourishment. Imagine his soft head and forming limbs pressed against the massive solid golden forepillar." (The head she refers to is now in my own hands in despair, thus making it impossible for her hands to remain. She lies beside me instead.) "For all we know, the amniotic fluid leaked away until its protective level was too low: poor Tommy may as well have beat his head against the wall as seek protection in that womb," says Sister, reenacting in dumb show my cranial trauma by adopting a modified fetal position and percussing the armrest of the Confidante with her own head. "It is no wonder that his brain is in a muddle!" (Thank goodness Mother has again slipped away.)

"Furthermore, to suckle while playing the harp wouldn't have been so very deleterious for Thomas, had she adapted her circumstance, for example by means of supernumerary mammae, supplying his needs by means of nipples perhaps on the thigh, as certain cases have illustrated, or an alternate site on her breast, even on the face or the back or the thigh—no, not the thigh— the disruption of pedaling—I had not taken that into account;

MARY CAPONEGRO

the slightest motion of the leg would jar an infant . . ." Sister begins to spin silently on the Jefferson Revolving Chair, the blur of her twirling causing her eyes to merge and gleam as one.

"A kind of enharmonic nursing?" Cecilia says soberly, in my direction.

"Nora, Daughter, it's no use. Please don't carry on. Thomas is denied his application money—and"—a withering glance toward Cecilia—"his secondary request. He has wasted my time again and made a mockery of the games, on this most sacred occasion of the year of Thomas Alva's death."

Cecilia looks at Father, repelled; Nora flustered, alarmed, panicked. I, to distract myself, echo Nora's gesture, by sitting before Ramelli's 1588 Rotary Reading Desk and rotating the wheel of useless books, more and more rapidly.

"No, Thomas, the invention fails. It is not approved; it offers no substance. Case closed! So let's go to the kitchen. Let's talk protein. If the brain must starve, at least the stomach can find satisfaction."

The change of scene should be a great relief—cooped up as we have been the evening long in the parlor—but there is no relief in store for Thomas Edward Smalldridge. How can I look at my fiancée? How can I ever face her again?

As we file in, funereally, to the L-shaped kitchen, Cecilia notes, more dutifully now than enthusiastically, "Oh my, isn't this a compact tabletop gas range—I've only heard about them. It must be brand-new—they can't have been available for long." Then I watch her trying to make sense of the array of random appliances, culled from disparate periods of invention's history: Carre's Artificial Ice Machine (the refrigerator's prototype) beside Rumford's Built-in Roasting-Over Range (with Rotary Plate) beside the Copper Tub. I lack the will to explain.

She bends to examine the fully electric kitchen range, noting that every saucepan has its own outlet.

"It's from the Columbia Exhibition," says Father proudly (with the same pride as if Mother had said, "it's from Paris"). But how long until Cecilia realizes there is no sauce in any saucepan, cranberry or otherwise, nor bird in the rotisserie—no function for any of these appliances designed to function.

"Never mind the gadgets, pretty lady, we'll get to the those. We're systematic in this house, and we have to start from"—with a pathetic, self-aggrandizing gesture he takes the box of kitchen matches, removes one and strikes its red head to make a sudden blue flame—"scratch. Fire is the basis for all cooking. Tell me how fire has become more controllable and accessible, Thomas? What advance has mankind made from two sticks rubbed together?"

But I am distracted by a vision of Edison's jam-packed head igniting from the heat of a lightbulb going off inside it so very frequently, idea after brilliant idea. I see the memorized photo of him, head in hand after five nights straight in front of the phonograph, the one upon which Father forced me to gaze so long as penance that my eyes played tricks upon me: the whole head bursts apart, reassembles, implodes again. Other times I see T.E. rubbing it against his desk as if to "strike" it, poor head streaked

MARY CAPONEGRO

with red instead of a match head's customary tracks of frictive white, his matchstick body emaciated after five days of inadvertent fasting—a novel way, wouldn't you agree, to beat one's head against the wall?

Then not exactly all the tea in China, but all Asia's bamboo ignites into a forest fire, whose flames whoosh all the way across the globe, singing SDRUCCIOLANDI, a cosmic cry—or is it a fiery finger glissing down a harp-strings' scale as each note blazes its incendiary resonance?

"Between now and the time you blow it out you should be able to tell me the history of its origins."

I am brought back abruptly from reverie to the threat of the present. How hard is it to remember two simple facts? 1892—book matches invented by Joshua Pusey. I blurt it out. But who bought the patent? Think.

"Ups the ante some, Son," says Father, of the flame at my fingertips. "Your scientific sister could explain to you how adrenaline speeds up the mind's ability to think, to move." (Then tell me, Father, Sister, better someone unrelated, why is my adrenaline molasses?)

"A singed finger might signal to the world in as salient a manner as a precious gem," intones Eleanor, persisting even as I undergo my torture to address my original, ill-fated request in maddeningly circuitous manner—until I recognize her succor in disguise; she is not simply repeating herself, she is reminding me the company is diamond.

"The Diamond Match Company in 1895."

To give her ruse more credibility (or out of habit), she continues, "But in such a case the flesh-inscribed ring would resemble the crude incisions made by those who call themselves blood brothers—and of course, no union can ever approximate the bond of blood."

"Now then," Father takes the reins again (and riding crop), "before we get to heat, to cooking, there are preliminary steps. Isn't it true Tom-Ed, that we can peel four-legged creatures just the way we peel a piece of fruit?"

"Yes, that is true, Father. In fact, the history of how the fruit is peeled would be the perfect festive subject to prepare for our repast."

"Not exactly what I had in mind. You could peel a pig as quickly as an apple, right?"

"The image of an apple in a pig's mouth is a familiar one, Father. Apples, in point of fact, have been the inspiration for numerous inventions of the previous century. I would be only too happy to tell you of them. In fact, the great Thomas Edison bet a barrel of apples that his invention . . ."

"Don't trivialize Thomas Alva's life by bringing up such stupid details."

"Are you all aware that a diabetic can be identified by the odor of apples about his person?" Eleanor adds. But her contributions do not, of course, qualify as "stupid details" even as she sniffs about the kitchen, presumably in search of hidden orchards, blooming from the soil embedded in the countertop's crevices. But her associations cannot spare me for more than a moment.

MARY CAPONEGRO

"As you wish, Father. Perhaps you consider it more relevant that Eli Whitney (who as you well know is associated, by a pedestrian public, with the cotton gin alone), when only thirteen, devised the first apple parer, in the eighteenth century. But one must note that he also made and repaired violins. And practiced law."

. "Get on with it, Thomas."

"Very well. In 1838 the apple is pierced with a fork, then rotated, then drawn and quartered by a four-bladed knife, and finally cored. The frame is wood. Then in 1869 the wood becomes iron and an automatic blade . . ."

"ENOUGH!!!" says Father, as if his head, like Edison's, would explode.

"But you . . ."

"Thomas, you're boring me, and even your polite little guest is yawning. Besides, that's not what I asked. We're past apples and eggs now. Get me to flesh. Be man enough to tell me how you can cram a cow into a can."

"Yes Father, courtesy of St. Armour" (my blasphemy elicits a disgusted look) "with Wilson's original patent #161,848 on April 6, 1875—corned beef cans and so forth . . ."

"'And so forth' does not qualify. Tell me how a pig is poked to prod it into service . . . come now, Tom boy, last chance, spit it out."

LADIES AND GENTLEMEN, FOR YOUR REVULSION *I am duty-bound to present to you a vision of the future: the* HOG HARP, *otherwise known as the Hamstrung Harp. Gut strings are favored by numerous instruments; why should this be modified to wire? When this instrument's famous ethereal sound begins to wear thin, a change of pace is achieved with the Hog Harp, which takes its design straight from our city's local pride: meatpacking. Lined up in a perfect row, as if hanging from a train-car ceiling, the creatures are stretched as taut as their flesh and muscle allow, at the brink of dismemberment, to make a dull thudding twang when the fingers, never singly but in solidarity, sound the thick distended strings by slapping. Pitch is barely a feature, remaining instead in the mind. No home possessing such a centerpiece would be forgotten.*

"With all due respect, Father, I prefer we concentrate on eggs and the eggbeater."

"Tom, it's exactly because of that preference that no one will ever respect you, and I will consider it highly disrespectful to me if you carry on with this kind of nonsense! Men have no business with eggs, Tom. Ask your sister for an anatomy lesson to prove it!"

She tugs at my sleeve like a child: "Tommy, come, we can be quick. Father gave permission, Tommy."

She virtually drags me to the pantry, starting, as in the bath-room earlier, to lift her skirt the moment we are sheltered. Can she really think her younger brother needs at twenty-five years of age a lesson in the facts of life? When I again prevent her, she hands me oleomargarine, a hint, I assume, at inventions with which I might deflect Father's single-mindedness. I realize I have left Cecilia vulnerable to his badgering; I cannot leave her alone with Father despite her greater courage and abilities. Now Nora has taken a paring knife from the drawer. To rip her clothes? For me to stab her dead? I'd sooner use it on myself at this point. Oh Sister, what demented scheme? Perhaps something more light-hearted: to excise carob nuts from the ear lest at any moment she commence hopping? This cannot be, I remind myself, what it appears. The cryosphinx has many guises.

"Help me to assist you, Brother. Give me a hand and I will give you all you need."

This is beyond my endurance, and my comprehension. With one hand I pull down the ever-upward-creeping skirt and with the other take firmly her arm, exiting the pantry. Oh, for the virtues of small talk. Where are those playing cards now? How can I attend to dear Cecilia? Anything for distraction.

"Cecilia, let me show you a modification I made of the 1860 version of the eggbeater for Mother—that's patent #30,053, Father—I strung harp strings in place of the gauze wire to make Mother a tiny harp-like eggbeater, a novelty item, you might say, just a souvenir, it was not one of my presentations."

"But it may as well have been," Father bellows before she can respond. "She's smart enough to see that by now. Which one of his presentations, I'd like someone to tell me, hasn't been a novelty item, a trinket? Eleanor, you're his champion, you tell me." Another rhetorical question, as he leaves her no opportunity to reply. "Your mother gave the boy the mistaken impression that life is one big party, with nonstop chat and idle leisure—no matter how much education I provide. And as penance you will tell me, Thomas, the answer to the question I asked you, about the pig."

"You refer, I believe, Father, to the Pig Killing Apparatus, for catching and suspending hogs. Six hog-trap patents in 1872 . . ." What choice is there but to obey, so I play along, repulsed by my own explanation of how the pig was scraped mechanically through a system of levers and pulleys, removing hair and bristle from its softened carcass.

Cecilia looks more and more sallow, her cheeks draining of the very color one associates with the pig. Poor pig. Poor pig.

"But if I might suggest, Father, given tonight's special company, perhaps we might concentrate on oleomargarine and baking powder, on eggbeaters and apple corers." I glance at Nora for affirmation.

"Don't bore me with more eggbeaters!"

"Thomas," Cecilia whispers weakly, even as she steadies herself with my arm, "don't change anything for my sake. What you must bear I'll bear too."

"I follow you, Tom boy. You want to stick with domestic inventions, suitable for mixed company. But hey, a woman who isn't tough shouldn't marry a loser in the worst year of u.s. history, am I right? Nora, am I right?" (My sister bows her head and does not answer. To my surprise she turns to my fiancée, offering her a covered burner on the 1858 cast-iron cooking stove to sit on.) "And I can tell you all, I'm sick to death of eggbeaters!"

"If pork makes you squeamish, Miss Crittenden," Sister offers, "perhaps poultry is more palatable. The great advantage to the latter is that thanks to the Frenchman, Reamur, it can be raised at any time of the year, due to the convenience of the 'Artificial Mother.'"

"Is it true, Thomas? Such a quaint title."

"Oh yes, Cecilia, such an invention does exist; there was a hot room for hatching, a cylindrical stove, a box lined with lamb's fleece and a ceiling inclined to imitate a hen's wings! But the French debt here may be to the Egyptians, who gave us the key and the harp."

"The French influence, as we know,"—Eleanor raises her voice shrilly toward Mother, now ensconced upstairs. Fool I am, why did I lay the bait?—"encourages time spent in other pursuits than maternal ones! Yes, an Artificial Mother, it seems to me, can be applied to any number of species. Not only fowl can profit from such surrogacy."

LADIES AND GENTLEMEN, *a softer proposition, an invention of fabric, the* HARP COVER, *on the model of Reamur's Artificial Mother's Hen-Wing Ceiling: in sum, a cover made of feathers to protect the harp at night and between playings. Like Reamur's ceiling that was all wing, all flight, this cover too enfolds the instrument in such soft, delicate nurture and protection that no one need consider it abandoned while not being played. Thus the harp has mothering in stasis as well as in activity.*

"The French are terribly clever, Miss Crittenden," Eleanor continues. Not surprisingly, it was a shrewd French baker who was the first to put his bread out earlier in the morning than was customary, earlier than all his competitors, leading to the tradition of night baking. (Baking is not as benign as you'd suppose, for we tend to forget that it requires a rotting body to make bread rise.) What's more, have you ever heard of the butcher called La Coupia, who killed animals using no other weapon than the pressure of his fingers?" (I feel a hand grasp mine and smile, then realize it is not my fiancée's.) "All the more brutal, one feels, for its subtlety—but perhaps ultimately a more merciful form of annihilation than that effected by dissembling fingers . . ."

"Nora, must you?" I ask, referring to both furtive gesture and public speech.

As if I hadn't entreated her, she barely takes a breath: "Fingers whose motion only the naive consider suggestive of rippling water or flickering light. There is nothing delicate or ethereal about pressing the fingers' flesh into strings themselves stretched taut over an obscene gold frame, Miss Crittenden, every eighth one blue, my brother claims, as an arbitrary marker,—each F could just as well be green—but I say it represents a vein, just as each C is not by chance blood's color. Beauty makes a subtle beast, doesn't it, Miss Crittenden? A kind of beast perhaps so well-disguised that it can only be recognized by examination of its waste?"

"Nora, Sister dear, I must inform you, our gathering is not the place for your poem."

MARY CAPONEGRO

Father counters, "And the Patent Office is not the place for yours, Son, resubmitted year after year, in all its shallow . . . immaturity. Do I make myself clear? Now, then—explain the abattoir in depth. Immediately."

But I gag on the brutal facts, assuaging myself with memories of the slender solace that Eleanor and I had through play. My mother once explained to us Napoleon's private abattoir called "La Vilette," and Sister and I made our "La Vilette," in Wilmette, Illinois: an iron and glass stall imagined from humble props within our bedrooms. In lieu of the pillow fights that mark giddy children's bedtime antics, Sister and I would fashion a dance of death between animal and human partner, the two not ever on equal footing. "NEXT, NEXT, NEXT," we would dispassionately shout. She would deliver the blow with the soft pillow-cum-mallet and I would feign the dire and instantaneous effects—fall backward onto the bed while she, her duty done, expressed compassion, stroking with tender palm the very place she had assaulted with the ersatz weapon. We would utilize two parts of a room to create our suite for suffering, alternating victim with murderer, as harp music offered strange accompaniment. "Poor beast," we sighed to one another, as we traded places, "poor beast," stroking each other's heads and horizontal backs as we received, on all fours, these condolences.

Then she hoisted me up onto the borrowed coat tree which stood in for the gambrel upon which an animal was hung. Once suspended, I would unbutton my shirt to allow her to reach in and pretend to extract organs from my innards. "You must give me your heart, poor beast; surrender your liver, you won't feel it." Again we traded places. Then into the bathtub each of us went, in turn, to be hosed with imaginary water.

But something has altered, gravely, in the period of time between our childhood play and this night. Something I am always seeking to understand, and remain haunted by—just as I cannot banish the head of Marie Antoinette from my imagination, divided from her body, apt metaphor for how circumstances forced her to divide her time between the State and the harp. As far as Father is concerned, she who bid her subjects eat cake received her just desserts! Strangely enough, the Queen's harp was imported to Brooklyn of all places, via Sweden. Why then not all the way to the purlieus of Chicago? I feel it moving closer, as if each night it floated further west; it might stand in our very house years after we have perished, not only every c but every note, each time-besotted string, streaked red.

"I need an entrée, Tom!" Father bellows.

"And I have lost my appetite," Cecilia whispers.

"Do tell us, Father," Nora says, "of the Columbia Exhibition."

And so we go, anecdotally, to the World's Fair of Chicago 1893, as we have many times before, to save our skins—for that event is his Achille's heel, a way to "buy time," as the saying goes, when Father cannot be appeased. Eliciting his nostalgia is our only respite, and that event his only vehicle for sentiment.

"The whole Columbia Exposition was a university for me," he explains, on cue, "I was self-educated. No one handed me the tools I needed. The exhibition raised the standards for all patent furniture," he then reminds us, "and the architecture itself was magisterial." (Fortunately he is so enamored of his memories that he does not notice Mother's sarcastic whistle from the top of the stairs, nor Cecilia's earnest comment that a distaste for the European-influenced architecture enshrined there was the catalyst for Mr. Frank Lloyd Wright's American originality, an impulse she would imagine Father would endorse.) Father was mesmerized most of all, of course, by the renowned sleeping car display. His teary-eyed remembrances make me want to take out my imaginary violin, but of course there would be consequences for the ridicule.

We hear, again, how he wanted to sleep on the premises, ideally in the sleeping car itself, even though the train was not, obviously, in motion. He begged the officials to hire him as a tour guide, and then moved, with the train, when the time came, to the rails, having found his calling (and his city). Explaining every feature of the train's latest improvements to the crowds was sheer exhilaration, as close as he could come to living inside its genius. We hear how he he walked the length of each railcar hour after hour, inspecting every corner, every fixture, filled with awe, no less than if it were a chapel.

When his reverie is complete, he becomes sour again, chastises us. "But I know none of you would take my word for it, so I'll quote that intellectual, William James, who said he'd mortgage his soul to get there."

"Yes Hubert, the quote is James's, but I'm afraid he was

being sarcastic!" Mother, like a mirage, again in our midst. "However, we know yours is an earnest sentiment; we all know Hubert is a man who would mortgage his family in a minute to retrieve the sensation of . . ."

"Look who's talking," he interrupts. "Sensation is your god, not mine. Who hopped off to Paris every chance she had, abandoning us all? And for what great cause? To nibble at pastry and pluck!"

I see a hand glissing down the scale but breaking every string in turn, so that in the wake of its more customary sonority, each one snaps. What should be liquid becomes a waterfall of broken glass.

"Tell me, Thomas, can you name Chicago's entrepreneurial heroes, and state the sums that marked the beginning of their careers?"

Dutifully I parrot the sums: Armour migrating to California with one hundred dollars in his pocket in 1851, G. Hammond beginning a small meat shop with thirteen dollars cash and a fifty-dollar banknote, Swift beginning in New England with twenty-five dollars.

"Does that seem like a huge amount of capital, Tom boy?"

"No, Father, although . . ."

"What other obstacle did they face?—aside from getting from the East to the Midwest, which I took care of for you."

Even as I explain how Swift and Armour needed to con-

MARY CAPONEGRO

vince the railroads and butchers that they could supply a superi-
or cut at a lower price, the meat and train become in my mind
a single entity, each cow a freight car whose tail ties around the
neck of the cow behind it, thus gradually strangling it—a train
like long loaves of meat on wheels, a stench for miles of rotting
flesh. It gives me a sense of foreboding, to which I fear I may
have to surrender.

> LADIES AND GENTLEMEN, *the inventor begs you to
> indulge him a revision of the infamous* TUNING
> KEY/TEETHING RING. *The inventor has improved his
> modest device, eliminating a step of the process. Whereas
> before the user had to choose between one activity or the
> other, now she need not alternate; now one simple twist of
> the baby's head will tune her flattened string without
> interruption of teething. The device need never leave the
> baby's mouth. (And babies, whose forming bones are far
> more malleable than ours, will garner even greater flexibil-
> ity about the neck.) The musician can thus have her cake
> and eat it too, unlike Marie Antoinette, who could not
> both eat cake and have her head.*

Edison's gold-molded records from Orange, New Jersey, "echo
all over the world," as does his success—and its corollary: my
shame. The cylinder that houses one such record sits on my desk;
I scrutinize it daily. Why doesn't Father find the cursive flourish
that makes a canopy atop the T in the great one's signature a sissy
gesture? Why doesn't he see, like me, the T become a gibbet with
a hanged man suspended on either side of its crosspiece? And

why doesn't he hear, as I do, in that international echo, the cries of all the slaughtered animals who have succumbed to mankind's ingenuity? As to the gold-framed columns of red-printed numbers (dates of patents with others pending)—it might as well be my blood they are penned in, or that of cattle branded with them. In spite of the great one's sober gray face rimmed by a decorative gold oval, the poor beasts march inexorably to slaughter, perhaps because of him? His gray face watches impassively over this butchery.

"The money, granted, was modest . . . but Swift was not swift, Father. We remember him for the first successful storage refrigerator, of 1882. But we do not necessarily recall the twenty years of failure that led up to it! Nor is he alone. Your friend Fuller waited fourteen years between applying for and receiving a cash register patent. Morse as well waited an eternity for approval, and let us not forget his true aspiration, art!"

"There's a difference, though, Tom: their failures or their obstacles were overcome, and led eventually to success! That is the drama of their story. Yours is monotonous, trivial."

LADIES AND GENTLEMEN, *may I present, for the first time, an innovation to be used outside the home, for the protection of the entire property of the home-owner. For those who are troubled by unsolicited visits, or for that matter, for those who wish to discourage the exiting of the household's residents, the Musical Barbed-Wire Fence is a unique deterrent. While turned off it can in fact be plucked, so that*

MARY CAPONEGRO

getting a breath of fresh air need no longer be a severing from one's beloved instrument. Hands need not be idle as a constitutional walk around the yard is taken. However, if that walk is too long, or if the walker strays toward the street, the current running through the barbed-wire harp fence, when activated, (courtesy of Glidden's ingenuity) gives fingers a more strenuous calisthenic than had ever been intended.

"No, Thomas, you can't mean that it's almost midnight and you have nothing left to show for it! These jokes can't really be your idea of genuine inventions. Come tell me you don't mean it. Eleanor, he has a real invention, doesn't he? Tell me he has something. Something to make us faint instead of yawn! Has it all been completely worthless?"

"Yes, there is . . . something," cries Eleanor, "and here it is," with even more intensity than usual in her voice and manner. She throws herself at Father's knees, entreating him, then casts herself face-down across the fringed, overstuffed Ottoman called the Pouf, hoisting her skirt up to her waist, too rapidly this time for anybody's intervention. Does my sister invite a beating, making herself a scapegoat for me? How can I allow it? And then I see the truth, for she lowers her undergarments to reveal between her buttocks an approximately five-inch length of cartilaginous protuberance—awe-inspiring really, in the manner of a meteor shower or eclipse or some celestial display visible only several times a century.

Her tail must have been sequestered for more than thirty years and no doubt pseudonymously exposed in print by Dr. Cranshaw in some obscure medical journal, to advance his career. Call me cynical, call me unfair, if I cannot help but hear the doctor/barker's voice: "Step right up, ladies and gents, only a dime, and see for your own eyes the caudal extremity, the human tail!" This voice competes in my head with that of Edison's famous recording of "Mary Had a Little Lamb"—the naughty version, thought shocking by some—although it is not Mary's calf we here behold but Nora's tail, far more shocking than any stream of words.

Now upon closer inspection, the whole evening comes clear, for at the base of the appendage, I observe the curious effect of mica in pavement—a patina quite incongruously allied with flesh. I must squint—as did Eleanor, for my sake, through the keyhole in her youth—to deduce at last, that the strange appearance derives from a tarnished gold band so snugly secured that the skin would appear to have grown over it, not unlike the bark of a tree over a girdling hoop. This ring, by now, could not be slipped off. It would require assistance to dislodge, and it would have to be pried off with a sharp implement—severed, in any case, with great discomfort, for the band and the caudal extremity are securely married.

Nora, Nora, my own poor little lamb, how much the greater would have been the verisimilitude in our private play-acted "La Vilette," though then your secret was probably a mere bud, not yet blossomed to full length. You wanted to help me

MARY CAPONEGRO

still, poor beast. You tried, however awkwardly, to grant my request. You have never wanted otherwise, for you have always been my ally.

And what of us? What of us? We are ill and woefully weary. Dawn is nowhere at hand, and there is so much history yet to be accounted for. Already we are nauseated, and the nebulous climax toward which we climb has yet to show its countenance. I do not have the power to articulate it, any more than one could whistle fog. Father remains unsated. Will he ever be sated? His insistence on precision mounts. How will we stave off exhaustion? What is to follow? Midnight is about to strike, a downbeat of apodictic force: a stroke both subtle and irrevocable, both like a guillotine's blade—that mechanism made by man to maul his fellow men—and like the pressure of fingers that can instantly, unostentatiously fell an ox. All through the country, at this moment, couples kiss, but I cannot solicit my beloved's tender lips, which might, in time—if time were kind—yield her tongue: organ she would now be loathe to mingle with mine, loathe even to imagine. It is at this moment clearer to me than ever before that even the wisest and kindest among us cannot bear to taste the truth of the meat we are.

Oh that I could lie upon lamb, find shelter in fowl, shrouded under its winged roof, bathe my eyes in utter darkness, and pour silence into my ears; that I could stay the onward rush of mechanization with some custom-blended stupefacient, stimulated by neither thought nor problem-solving, rising to no challenge, fielding no questions, immune to sequence, innocent of alphabet—and take, in particular, the increments of melody and harmony, and loosen their hold, their relational tenacity— untorque the tension of every instrumental string, until all lies lax and flaccid, and I too lie, purged of information of any kind, devoid of goal or responsibility, lie in my simple human skin and breathe the dark.

For their inspiration in the composition of her novella, the author is particularly grateful to the following two nonfiction texts: *Anomalies and Curiosities of Medicine,* by George M. Gould, M.D. and Walter L. Pyle, M.D. (Bell Publishing Company, 1896), and *Mechanization Takes Command,* by Siegfried Giedion (Oxford University Press, 1948).

MARY CAPONEGRO

EPILOGUE OF
THE PROGENY

— or —

Whoever Is Never Born
with the Most Toys Wins

Not to be born surpasses thought and speech.
The second best is to have seen the light
And then to go back quickly whence one came.
—SOPHOCLES, *Oedipus at Colonus*

I

See the boy in his bed, how he tosses and turns; his mouth trembles, eyes flutter beneath their lids, then stillness. Again, the same sequence. This boy, in a bed only recently become his, will hours later awake to the almost familiar: posters and knickknacks and trophies and photos, surroundings the boy does not see while he sleeps, while he dreams, a boy in his room in a comfortable house, which exudes, this particular morning, the aroma of bacon frying, an aroma in retrospect predictable.

Numerous mornings like this have occurred, and even though the boy's tummy still reeks of the cloying sweetness of too many shirley temples, the sputtering strips provide him incentive to exit his dreams and to transcend his nausea, which is, after all, only slight.

The boy then remembers the Bar in which he spent the previous evening, and the evening before that, and so on—a Bar more familiar than this room, which is as it happens the boy's favorite color—although for a passing moment it becomes his least favorite. As he lies between these walls he feels repeating on him the many maraschino cherries he consumed at the Bar, in his nervousness, in his effort to disguise that very nervousness, as an adult might draw incessantly from a cigarette. He would in fact find himself holding the stem in just such a manner, between index and middle finger, even after he had pulled away the soft head of round fruit with his teeth.

The Bar he remembers as background for a woman's expectant face, her slightly parted lips, a man's clenched hands, his strong jaw, their solicitous antiphonal words, the glut of their persistence, his own weary acquiescence. Oh, what's the use of dwelling in the anguish of the morning after? You're here now, may as well get out of bed, go down the stairs, get on with it. Conveniently, no matter which evening or who, they always have the same name. Morning, Mom. Morning, Dad, the boy intones. Thanks for last night. Hey, smells great. Is this my place?

❧ II ❧

See the girl on the bench; she appears nonchalant, her head propped on her elbow like that, her cheek pressed against her palm. Is she gazing dreamily at the pond situated in front of this circle of benches, or does she turn to observe the chaotic ensemble behind her: the informal parade of potential parents who daily comprise a backdrop at least as compelling if objectively less scenic.

Perhaps it is not indifference but wistfulness the girl exhibits, as she continues to look on, intent on disguising her interest. Or her longing? By sunset it will be decided; the girl will go home with a mother or father, or more likely both, unless she elects, one might say, by default, to go home to the parents whose house she awoke in this morning, the parents who tentatively kissed her good-bye as she left for that Park, and who are perhaps themselves defensive participants, as it were, in the informal procession of persons, possessions, and gestures. These pending parents, if espied by the girl, might shrug as if to say, we have to watch out for ourselves, for our future, we have to insure against loss. For all they know, the girl may exit the Park holding the hand of the woman who at this moment displays a slender cylindrical metal artifact, made gold by the sun, which she then pulls apart into glistening halves.

As the girl squints at the cylinder held to eye level, the woman sustains her captive audience by causing to rise up from the base a creamy bright finger. This gesture received by the girl is equivalent to the woman's own beckoning index. The brightness of its erected color, particularly in relation to the gold tube from which it emerges, is mesmerizing, for it is a color to which one is obliged to attend, a color which recalls to the girl the fire engines that had delighted her in earlier years, and which, if she were lucky, she would discover in miniature version sequestered in a stocking of the same hue affixed to a random fireplace in proximity to a decorated evergreen on what would become the most anxious day of the year.

⌐ III ⌐

All days resemble that day in their way. All days are parcels in which gifts are wrapped, gifts to a child from a parent, some more mysterious than others. Even now, in the park, parents stroll bearing gifts, and which gift can determine which child. Perhaps the girl will accompany the couple who balance between them the cage of a gerbil, setting it down on the opposite end of the bench, the better for her to witness its occupant's antics. She surveys his sparse furnishings, watches as he mounts the diminutive wheel and sets himself in confined motion. The tip of her index finger taps at the bars after she surrenders her veneer of indifference. Coochie coo, little guy. (In reply, his whiskered face approaches hers from the other side, as if even this creature were schooled in seduction.) In all likelihood they will allow the pet to be housed in her room, the room about to become her room. And whatever name it is her whim to call the gerbil will become the word by which all call it. Thus the girl has no new names to learn other than those of her creating once she whittles her options down to one: Oh thank you, Dad, thank you, Mom. And bucky thanks you too. Mind if I close the door now?

⌐ IV ⌐

Thousands of such transactions occur in the Park; thus its surroundings are ultimately irrelevant. No one, in fact, attends to the

MARY CAPONEGRO

beautiful scenery, not to boats nor to swans, nor to trees, nor to their blossoms or leaves, nor does anyone tend to exhibit disgust at the sundry synthetic debris that accretes in the interstices of Mother Nature. Any unoccupied plaything, any artifact not in a child's hand, anything in storage long enough to gather dust is a time bomb of sorts, one that does not tick but sings, sings of failure, hiatus, unseemly gaps between one child and that child's successor. Recycling does occur from one child to the next, but along the way the mass of detritus mounts, since the traffic of parents and children naturally propagates excess. See the batteries left to corrode in the walkman, the camera, the radio, the windup toy? Toss them, then!

You can't see the nicad dying inside the computer, tape recorder, or toothbrush. Make sure you don't trip over tennis balls gone awol, dented classic coke cans—ah, what kid can resist just one kick?—unretrieved pacifiers, torn wash & dry packets, soiled squeaky toys, bent bubble-blowing wands. More abundant than any other item littering the park are cardboard and cellophane, the evidence of packages bought and opened in desperate haste, not by an eager or greedy child, but by an anxious parent primed for giving. Clearly, there isn't a moment to lose between toy store and park. Who could expect any self-respecting parents to pick up after themselves? Everyone knows they're here only to score.

V

Can you believe that man behind the catcher's mitt?—holding it coyly in front of his face like a mask, then lowering it just enough to let you see his eyes. He winks and lifts the bulky glove another notch again. "Play peekaboo with POOKY, pal. Give me a break and leave the props at home," you want to taunt, but instead mutter, under your breath, to the gang. "Pathetic!" heather hastens to confirm. "Just ludicrous," say tim and tom in unison, as much to mock megan, who learned the word last week at school and finds a niche for it in every other sentence, as to reinforce your disdain. But all of you know he's no less objectionable than the woman beside him bribing with her cleavage bait, a teething ring like some enormous gaudy piece of costume jewelry on her finger. Have they ceased discriminating altogether? Don't you look your age, for child's sake? You're not in diapers anymore. The guy is over-eager, pitching arm winding compulsively, give him the slip.

"Ditch him before he thinks he's made a conquest," mike urges. "Don't even look in their direction, don't encourage them," jen pleads. Eye contact, all of you concur, is the key to scoring parents or avoiding them. Look at anyone instead, even at the two adults stooped under the weight of the heavy aquarium—the extension cord attached to it tripping parental pedestrians right and left, who in turn accuse the bearers of ill intent, for a parent competing on crutches must obviously carry less—as the tank's darting shimmery occupants negotiate the murky sloshing waters, appearing to all who view them, even through the slime and algae'd sides, as if they'd have been better left at home.

MARY CAPONEGRO

Look at any of the burdened parents who trail behind them tricycles, dirt bikes, and bicycles, every so often a unicycle, cross-country skis, poles, and rollerblades—for it's common knowledge that the coup for all parents is to be the chosen one the day those training wheels come off, to have been the transitional couple in witness of that first liberating albeit still tentative glide down the block upon the single unsupported slender tread, one front and one behind, no unsightly anchored sides, two instead of four; they'll document in every medium available, boast eternally of this moment to their friends and share it with you again and again (and again and again) in the family room, on video, and as far as you're concerned—and tim and tom and jeff and mike and megan, jen, and debbie—you ought to make them work for it. It isn't something any family should be allowed to take for granted. How many milestones in one childtime are available for distribution, with so few unequivocally triumphant feats among the trial-and-error cumulative skills or less than glamorous exigencies, once one traces the trajectory from teething, speaking, crawling, sitting, shitting unassisted, walking, shoelace-tying, standing on one's head, masticating solid food, carving, spearing, scooping with utensils powered by oneself, and so forth, so on, on and on to the ceremonious if anxious acquisition and subsequent removal of braces, jock straps, and brassieres.

An enterprising couple flick a plastic orthodontic retainer tentatively, then get carried away and fling it back and forth as if it were a frisbee, from ever greater distances, until one fails to catch it, and the now soiled, even more unsightly item is

retrieved, brushed off furtively on a sleeve and returned sheep-
ishly to the woman's pocket. "EEUUWW," says jen. "Who knows
where it's been—how gross!" And debbie adds, "We know that
it's been on the ground, for one." But no child is ignorant of the
retainer's ramifications, i.e.: who among the array of candidates
assembled before them will pay for braces, glasses, ice cream, pets,
karate, circus expeditions, laptops, let alone the pièce de résis-
tance, college! Who can be persuaded NOT to pay for violin,
piano lessons, sewing, boxing, Sunday school, ballet . . . ? Your
friends trade endless interpretations of computer equipment: "It
means you'll never see them, they'll be at the screen all evening."
"Yeah, what's wrong with that? The perfect setup." "What's the
point of choosing them then?" "That's the point, you jerk. You
never have to deal." "No, it means you move in and it's yours;
you're at the screen all week!"

Endless ambiguities, endless predictions, suppositions, intuitions, concerning the wielding of razors, insertion of tampons, siz-
ing of brassieres. (Parents' magazines now disrecommend bras as
props precisely because of ambiguity. The interpretation "We won't
procrastinate, won't hinder your entry into womanhood" is as easily read as "You had better keep your breasts confined. Your body's
freedom is your parents' jurisdiction." Not for long, of course.)

Just because they enter the arena with an arsenal of shuttle-
cocks, sailboats, and soccer balls, frisbees, action figures, dolls, and
teddy bears and pop-up books and rollerblades, walkmans, running shoes, dresses, T-shirts, levis; croquet mallets, wickets, legos,
minibikes, and nautilus equipment—"Look," says jen, "today the

MARY CAPONEGRO

caboose is an iguana!"—does that entitle them to trophies gratis? You want to insinuate subliminally from a loudspeaker hidden in the park's tallest tree, you want to bellow in shrill chorus with all of your accomplices, "There's no such thing, dear mom, dear dad, as a free child!"

Chant it daily and don't give in. Don't get soft. Never play other than hard-to-get. On the other hand, remember that once you're entangled you cannot truly extricate yourself; you're in the clutches of a gradual suffocation, this one, that one, no one with the right to say, "stay here," and so you're free to go from house to house but driven to keep looking to avoid the unbearable realization that it might very well have been better—certainly simpler—never to be born.

~ VI ~

Duck, duck, duck, duck, GOOSE! You have no hiding place. Accept your crowning syllable with dignity. Don't squawk with indignation at the unexpected sentence levied by a gleeful, careless palm. The crude, unsavory cadence that seals your fate at playtime becomes in dream an absurd noise that issues from the throat of the void. Is that what you want, say the nightmares that wake you gasping, your torso at a sudden right angle to the cot in your current parents' den, never to be born? Not to have been born? "Yes, just a bad dream," she coos, the new one soothing you, cradling your head in her arms, while your nose is scrunched against the very breast that could as easily have been nurturing another, its stiffened tip wedged into the mouth of itty-bitty, bald and pudgy, toothless Pooky, had the barstools been differently arranged, had the times been slightly skewed, had your eyes followed a different route—and yet they were not, things are as they are: you two ensconced as if you'd formed yourselves this way night after night, since time began, as if the rhythm of your fear were all moments pulsing in her being.

"My silly goose," she says, when you, without defenses yet, in hypnopompic haze, confess the title of your fright from which she fortunately dares not extrapolate. "You're not in trouble, silly goose," she soothes, "you're in a cozy quiet safe red room, with nothing to be frightened of." (What won't allow this to be true? Her soft strong arms and tenderness almost break through something even stronger in you. Where is its release?) Concerned that she has been dismissive of the shadow that still folds you, yet emboldened nonetheless, her tenderness augments, ends in a sibilance far more solicitous than the bird's name that assaulted you, then pierced your sleep and bid you scream.

You dare not disappoint her, dare not shatter her illusions, with the weighted truth that is your private grief. It must be so that every child who stayed here had the same disease. The sheets are fresh, the mattress not infested; something subtler even than the air and as pervasive bears the spores of your malaise. Such is your fate: to know the sheets will be forever fresh, the bed only almost familiar, the parent in her earnest nurture unable to reverse your unrelenting inquiry as to whether it might be better had you never . . .

VII

"OK. Try not to think of a pink elephant," Father says to this week's daughter, a mischievous gleam in his eye. He is impressed with his playful challenge. What better way to break the ice than with a harmless inexpensive game whose sole equipment is imagination? As for the girl, her room is pink as is the dress laid out for someone's party, and the sheets and quilt as well, so it's even more difficult not to capitulate. The forbidden lures, a vast pink magnet.

"GOTCHA," Papa says, "I bet that guy got in your head!" "Yes, Papa," she replies. "Did you put him there?" Every five seconds thereafter, he puts his tongue against his teeth while pursing lips to simulate a buzzer (like a gameshow blooper sound) and presses index finger to her belly, then her upper arm like a pretend inoculation. "You thought of a pink elephant, didn't you?"

Indeed, she now can think of nothing else, even after perky daddy departs and shuts the door behind him. And the more she tries the more its weight crushes, its trunk begins to wrap around her neck, a scarf of pure muscle, its tusks indent her shoulders. The landscape of not being born should be spacious and weight-less, she considers, so why has it taken this form? Besides, isn't this what parents are supposed to protect you from?

Take off. This isn't working out. Stuff that dress in your pocahontas knapsack and find another party. This Papa is one busted prophylactic.

VIII

Why do you feel somehow akin to the pet who maneuvers predictably on his tiny wheel, despite the fact that you've seen a hundred hamsters, just as many gerbils, toucans, parakeets, canaries, goldfish, finches, silver dollars, wooden nickels, stamp collections, comic books with every single superhero, and just when you're thinking it's been a while since you've seen—an iguana? By now pam and heather and debbie can be relied upon to roll their eyes whenever you spy a cage. "What a cliché!" megan complains.

Yet these reluctant affinities persist. You feel more kindred to the furry creature than you do to jeff and mike, even as you scoff with them, for there's neither urge nor opportunity to confide in them, what's mingled is not feeling, it is circumstance, they're only friends, you didn't choose them, after all.

Fate was your engineer. You stood unwittingly on one site, they on another, and from that moment on it was clear you would be cruising together. Your relation remains the product of who stood where when. Based on this alone, you are destined to watch each other grow stubble and muscle, and over time deepen the timbre of your speech, just as megan and debbie and heather will swell at hip and chest, as you discuss in exactly the same mode and manner each week the vicissitudes of family planning. Every one of you holds selective standards, but in the end, you can't afford to look down on anyone, can you? No one dares linger too long unattached.

When old-fashioned parents cajole you into playing hot potato, you find yourself uneasy, determined to win. You can't

MARY CAPONEGRO

bear to be caught at game's end with the spud in your hand. "What's wrong, howard? It's a harmless root vegetable; it isn't old, it isn't growing eyes yet." Yet through it, you can't help but see the prospect of annihilation. You flee to your familiar cluster and commence preaching at them in a most uncharacteristic manner.

"We call them pathetic," you begin, "the parents who are the object of our never-ending search." You find yourself projecting like a child possessed, to a congregation comprised of an unwilling tim and tom and debbie, heather, jen, and mike. "But are we any less? Perhaps we only appear to have the upper hand!" "Oh, lay off, howard, find a family," heather retorts. Disgusted, tim and tom add, "Yeah, how, go get homed."

IX

So home you go, and get there just in time for a piano lesson, on the magnificent instrument that lured you to this house in the first place, despite its wretched name. Baby grand. If you could learn just one tune, you might console yourself with it on any spinet, any upright in a hallway or a basement of the houses yet to come. EVERY GOOD BOY DOES FINE, writes Mr. Pultney, for probably the hundredth time this month. If only life were so simple as the lines on the staff paper claim. The bass clef's letters tell you nothing new, they just make the treble's message plural—in case you forgot, between the staves, what good boys do. And furthermore, they do it into perpetuity.

The only trouble is, when Mr. Pultney drills you on the basics, demonstrating that the half steps, E to F and B to C, break up the pattern of the C Major scale, you can't persuade your fingers to make the leap from 3 to 4 and 7 to 8; you want to seal those vast white spaces up, or stick a sharp or flat in there. "It's just a half step, howard," he assures you, "like the others," but it's too late. The keyboard you had hoped to conquer in one afternoon has become an ivory sea expanding asymmetrically. You can't tell Mr. Pultney that the structure of the music keeps reminding you to wonder whether you were ever born.

X

You'll never have a song; you should have known. Even when Mr. Pultney made a whole note chord to fill in every space of the treble staff and called it FACE, you saw instead a stack of bald heads from the back that could belong only to the competitor: that baby, with his mindless smile. What a cheap come-on; he'll favor anyone who shoves a toothy grin under the decadent awning of his imported collapsible stroller. Those sounds out of his mouth: a gooey syrup any kid would be ashamed to ooze. As if to give a clue, his mouth often shapes itself into a tiny "o." But a parent, shameless, oozes even more unctuously than an infant. See how the latter is fondled by the former with exotic unguents for his belly button, as if a tree above his groin had been uprooted, and now they have to fertilize the soil with utmost care. Further down grows a sapling newly peeled of bark, likewise tended to alleviate rawness, and then, as if that weren't enough, they flip him over on his painstakingly assembled changing table to assuage his chafed buttocks. Why not a kiss for each cheek while they're at it?

MARY CAPONEGRO

Cream him till he heals, the lucky dog. Tend his tiny pecker day and night. You envy those transient wounds less for the nurture they elicit than for the badge they make, for no scraped knee or band-aid; no slinged arm or cast or crutch could ever provoke the slavish fascination that baby's wounds command.

These sites upon his flesh are semaphores. See how they demarcate what time's compulsive healing will dissemble: the choice to barter doubt for an assumption that it's better to be born. (Oh if only you too could participate, could surrender doubt. What went awry with you?) Once these decorations are removed by time, the option of imagining an alternate to what apparently exists is rubbed away as well. (Yes, soon the wound will be invisible; you'll search in vain as for a contact lens on carpet or an earring in the yard or a tarnished key in soft new-fallen snow over an unlit driveway; you'll search each inch of baby-skin to find only an unmarred perfect surface, no residue of trauma, no souvenir of the potential superiority of avoiding being born.)

Of course the parents yearn to be the ones erasing. Or else they stand themselves to be erased! (And he, beloved babe, as ignorant as his admirers, will be duped. Who will correct him?) A flash of inspiration. Simple as that, the formulation comes to you: a baby is favored for being contiguous to nothingness. A baby is obsessively attended so that what most profoundly marks him can be all the more expediently hidden for posterity.

Is the glass half-empty or half-full? (A parent's favorite trick-question.) Is the baby in his almostness a catalyst for despair or celebration? Depends on whom you ask. You would undoubtedly be crowned the pessimist, given your intuitions, which might be formulated as follows: if jen and tim and mike and debbie, heather, tom, and you could nonchalantly lift your shirts or tug your waistbands that crucial inch to unveil a pride of belly buttons, and in so doing manifest a scar commemorating entry into this preposterous theater, none of you would need to flip through pages of arresting if occasionally off-putting images or to gossip or to gamble for your immediate futures or to patrol, as if a predator, the public places that are closer, in a real sense, than any house you've ever shacked-up in, to home.

XI

Meanwhile in the Bar, in the Park, in the Mall, the clichéd questions persist. You supply your share, because you know you can't be more original yourself, a slave to habits, patterns every child inherits. How many have you had? (A question uttered as if it hadn't been a thousand times already.) For some the higher number is the greater swagger; others, more mature, honor the lowest integer with a whistle of awe, as if to say, you must be doing something right. You all, in theory anyway (in speech at least), abjure the bars, but continue to populate them night after night, day after day, with heads bowed or eyes lowered in shame (averting each other's gazes), but never failing to note an exit. It isn't merely gossip-lust; it's a pragmatic way of keeping track, since updating an address book is a futile task. The next day, gossip will proliferate: who bought whom a glass of milk? Was skim or 2% on tap? "But what a tap at home!" shane nudges you, and gestures

MARY CAPONEGRO

toward the baby who, in view of all, roots at a woman's barely covered breast before they're even out the door.

Or was that the night—or week—before? Well that's shane, ever-immature. You can't do more than roll your eyes at him, even though he's in a different clique; for that matter you can't do more for tim and tom and jen and debbie, that's how it goes with friends, it's not as if you choose them. shane's still in the inchoate stage, he reads the juvenile magazines; he isn't weaned off *PLAYMOM* yet, for child's sake. You'd just as soon avoid him, but of course, he's in the same rat-race; you have no choice, fate put you in that same spot side by side at the bar to endure the tedious gossip while you sip your sixteenth shirley temple. Who went where with whom, for one night, one week, surreptitiously or proud, enthusiastic or indifferent, but in all cases advising each other, as if advice were not irrelevant, as if advice could make a difference, warn against, for instance, the tendency to succumb to TOYS-B-US, to glaze over at the glitz of a beach ball or stroller or swing.

Don't think no strings attach, that nonexistent voice will never say, to your new gift, you're going home with them to try it out, together, for the camera, for posterity. Watch them assemble it, poking holes in the ground to secure the poles, attaching the crossbar to secure your weight. Hear their squeals of delight as you seat yourself, receive their push, and then pump dutifully, dispassionately, perfunctorily; if enough momentum accumulates to raise you parallel to earth they clutch each other's waists in glee, but if you carry on too vigorously they'll be alarmed. After a spate of families, going through the motions is like second nature, though admittedly an enervated nature. You'll swing for your supper tonight, for tomorrow's you'll pitch, play parcheesi, or poker, charades, guide them through the cd-rom inherited from your predecessor without the least awkwardness to taint your enthusiasm, and of course the old standby, the tube, the cave into which the whole family can climb without any exertion, still attached to the couch.

"And how many times during that week," they'll ask you next time in the Park (mike, megan, heather, debbie, tim, and tom) "did you watch TV together, and what was the size of the set, how many controls on the panel and where, and who was in what position on the couch, were you between them?" Most crucial question: "who held the remote? Was it you who chose the program every time?" (It's always that way at first, some say.)

And who can say what intangible ennui impels you to go on and seek the next set, next sofa, the next ping-pong table— whose paddles can double as both punitive and recreative objects, so certain families, you notice, in the park, have stopped using them as props. "The cowardice of exploiting ambiguity," say debbie, jen, and heather (recently obsessed with ethics), for instance, when couples flash the paddles in the park to double their yield among those who crave discipline (after several lax situations) and those who read their presence as promise of endless play.

"Is every toy an oxymoron?" megan asks. "Save that for school, OK?" says tim. tom nods. "So what, though," you propose, "if parents send mixed signals or if children misinterpret? Every family is a gamble; don't you get it? Next week always brings

MARY CAPONEGRO

another chance. They're playing poker up the block tonight; scrabble across the street. It's less exciting in the place where I crashed yesterday; would you believe—don't laugh—old maid? The stakes are just as high though." The only tragedy would be to sit too long at the table with that hag or that fool in your hand; just deal again, my friend, just deal again, get to the next game, at the next house, before you start to question if you were ever born.

⌒ XII ⌒

Every child needs respite. Go on. Lay your body across the beat-up billiard table; don't bother about the small damp spot your cheek leaves on the worn felt. Go ahead, roll the ball down the length of the table just to hear it thud into a corner pocket, just to feel release from the exertion and the sound. You're doing it again, you're doing it again, and what other choice is there but to carry on, unless you elect to cease to be.

At the end of a long chain of effort and experiment might you surrender to the unbearable simplicity of never having been born? Anything's possible. But in the meantime, you will share the housewise smarts each of you have acquired through trial and error. At thirteen, for instance, declare you must go to a small prestigious liberal arts college, if not an ivy league university. You're hot. At seventeen aver that a state school or vocational institution are the only possibilities. Again you've got your pick of parents. Because if you don't shed your ivy league fantasy by the time the funds are required, you're not just hot, pal, you're a hot potato! When tuition time looms, their pride succumbs to penny pinching. Just as scissors cut paper and paper covers rock, frugality eclipses pride.

⟡ XIII ⟡

Why even complain to them, your friends? They won't understand. And nonetheless, too bored to sip your sixtieth shirley temple without some—even lame—conversation, you entertain your peer's complaint.

"Can you believe she used the same pet names for him as she did for me? I even overheard her cooing in the new one's ear, 'my precious.' Then she had the gall to suggest we take our bath together, placated by a stupid squeaking duck, while she put these dumb plastic halos on both our heads. 'See how fond I am of both of you,' she crooned, 'I buy the product guaranteed to keep away tears!'" (He bawls as he relates the irony.) "As if she hadn't made me cry in every other way."

"Chill, jamie. Don't take it so hard, huh? It's just one incident. One mom. Don't take it personally. You'll get a better set-up next time. We all get burned."

And then, oh dear, the object of his misery appears, and the scene begins. These occasional public confrontations do add drama to routine but hardly seem worth the humiliation. Familiar trepidation. Milk splashed in the woman's face. Then she reciprocates. Before you know it, jamie has raided your shirley temple, both his and your cherries dropped down her dress. He gets his wish: her tears. He loses patience, screams at her, "Go

bear your breasts in sight of someone new, since you're so greedy
as to want two. Most parents count themselves blessed to have
one and then one and then one! Why not go for twins?"—it's
getting ugly now. You move away instinctively. "How about those
infants in the corner? Hey everybody, watch and let us know
when they cry or yawn at the same time so my ex-mother gets
to stick both nipples in, two for the price of one." Turns back to
her. The slap. You saw it getting out of hand. What could you do?
You're getting out of here.

It's time to go home, not a new one either, not tonight, no
energy left to be on the rent. A finished basement is a special
prize, hard to leave behind. Enjoy it while you can. Lie there
again, in the cool dark, your cheek against the newly damp green
felt. The parents upstairs would no doubt be honored to witness,
in fact would lust to console, your rare tears, but what consolation is there for the realization that this wood, this floor, these
posters—props they selected to please you—make you feel in
fact bleaker? You'd rather turn your head or close your eyes or
even cry than see through the awkward guesswork, to know
these are the vestiges of children who preceded you: effluvia that
embody their proclivities, their fantasies, all of which by
definition must be transitory.

Suddenly you feel compelled to seize the unmarked white
ball and hurl it against the cushioned side of the table in fury and
sorrow, so vehemently that it skips off the ridge and drops with a
crack to the floor. That is why you are here: whatever that null
sphere stands for; not because of the table or the TV or her nipples

(which admittedly elicit a nostalgia you cannot ignore or erase) or their eager faces or their hearts or good intentions, or for that matter their desperation. It is only as antidote to this void that you chalk the cue, twisting clockwise, counter, clockwise, the tip of the stick into the hollowed chalky center of the paper-covered cube until the blue dust makes you choke, then in frustration aim only at what will yield the most noise, as if you could crack open emptiness.

Soon enough their concerned voices echo in the basement stairwell. "Is everything all right? Is it too cold down there, howard? Should we turn up the heat, dear?" Why bring them into it? Shame is the least of it. What consolation could they offer, trapped as they are in the same situation, destined to go forward unceasingly into one illusion after another. In the subsequent silence echoing your own, you infer their reevaluation of explicit endearment. Was it premature? they're wondering. One simple syllable. Should they have uttered it instead tomorrow? Between today and tomorrow is an incalculable difference.

⟞ XIV ⟝

You remember a past time when the hint of that nipple, the sight of that dip at the bodice of her dress, would have been like a magnet, as it must be for all the current babies. If you were once one, why is there no sympathy forthcoming? Why do you resent that they are less discriminating? Why do you so envy that soft-bodied baldy who'll put his tiny chubby hands out to anyone

MARY CAPONEGRO

who pokes a face into his bassinet? He is the root, or is what was the root, the closest to it. He is the ... oh forget it, who can stand to think about it?

~ XV ~

Alone among the blades of grass and dandelions, a decent yard, (a good catch, pam or jeff would say), you feel consoled; perhaps you'll park with these rents for a while. Their property, at least, is soothing—and then suddenly she comes to fetch you in, claiming ticks hidden there between the blades can make you sick. "Oh, for child's sake," you tacitly implore, "let me pretend the grass at least is innocent." Nothing is simple anymore. You can't even enjoy the consolation of this classic childical gesture. "See me," you want to say, "the boy. See boy do simple thing."

But instead you see yourself blowing the delicate threads of the dandelion's head to denude its thereafter useless stem with far more emotional investment than you possessed as a toddler, an infant, a pathetic toothless Pooky, if ever you were such. You'd just as soon scrape off his navel crust, rather than watch them fawn over his mound of earth, the venerated mons umbilicum. The tree that fell there can't be heard except in the bleak, silent night of a helpless child desperately scanning the broadest band of universal doubt, only to discover a low rumbling or high-pitched scream: a frequency audible only to you, only to you and to whomever wonders whether this can pass for being born. That stem once bound to earth, now wrenched, divested of its gossamer head, has no function and no place.

Find another flower then. Pluck one petal, then another, until the daisy is mere button, and you, the victim of your new toy's arbitrary starting point, do willingly consent to have this hitherto harmless lovely growing thing be arbiter of your fate: Move on. Don't move on yet. Move on. Don't move on yet. Was born, was never born. (Get reckless now: eight petals left.) BORN. BETTER NEVER BORN. BORN. BETTER NEVER BORN. BORN. BETTER. NEVER.

XVI

How does she know the candle's count is accurate? No matter. Don't think. Blow! Keep blowing, until all flame is extinguished. Then the games begin! Pin the tail on the donkey. Whoever is the birthday boy or girl goes blind for the occasion. Stands passive as the white cloth is tied around her head over her eyes. "How does it fit?" her mother asks. You want to answer, "all too well!" There is a clown providing entertainment, but even his painted nose and goofy orange hair and bright billowing overalls cannot temper the suspicion that all of this festivity is just as much disguise.

Well, this is something novel. The parent has assembled a birthday band to provide live accompaniment for the game of musical chairs. He must have scoured the neighborhood for this orchestra of children who have somehow managed a botched continuity of lessons. Even learning *Happy Birthday* can take more than a week, and despite a probable parental conspiracy demanding all instrumental teachers include it as their first assignment, a child on trombone might have played violin last month, and the flautist hasn't practiced since she left the house in which the music stand is a permanent fixture.

Who can blame her? (Your only lesson ended dismally when Mr. Pultney couldn't help but notice that the open sound of the perfect fourths and fifths he played to soothe you, on the contrary, exacerbated your anxiety.) Dutifully—or perversely?—the players accompany the other children's instinctive choreography: anxious pacing in a circle, like the gerbil in his cage or rat in a maze. Round and round and round. It would be too rude to put your hands over your poor assaulted ears. Each child plays in a different key, it seems, as the clown conducts with the long slender balloon he has blown up for the occasion. Your relief at the periodic cessation of cacophony is thwarted by the anxiety of knowing fewer and fewer chairs remain each time they pause. Can it be coincidence, you wonder, that the birthday girl or boy at every party is the first to be without a chair?

Yes, with babies it's simple: whichever parent inserts the pacifier first wins! So little nuance, scant discrimination. Even so, sometimes there are arguments about who got there first, and you want to say when you witness these squabbles, "why bother to argue? Why be competitive? Possessive for what? He'll be at your house in a week—or three months or a year, for rent's sake! Leave yourself something to look forward to." As with your friends, your so-called peers, who on occasion land together at the same house and don't exercise the courtesy of insisting "after you." "Can we afford this petty squabbling?" you demand of them.

Why do you play this role so often? Why can't they put their ears en masse to all the ticking toys surrounding them, why can't they hear the deafening song, why do you have to spell it out for *every*one? Sometimes there are seasons in sequence to boast of, but how often is that? Everyone knows that family photo albums don't even leave a discreet blank page between the children anymore. No kid gets all indignant even if she finds her photo smack against her predecessor's, on the same page. No kid who knows the score. No way! You don't stand on ceremony, you do your best to face the facts, but the one fact some can't seem to face is all the more elusive for its hypothetical status.

The sweet doughy face of a baby, for instance, insulates fact. Oh let them have their pacifier then. His parents will see a new face when he wakes them every other hour, that sweet yeasty mass contorted, scrunched in agony of lacto-lust or colic or teething or needing to be changed: an inchoate protest, and yet incipient acceptance of the realization that it would likely have been better never to be born.

⌐ XVII ⌐

A father stands in line with an infant strapped into his kiddy-sack—the kind designed for frontal carrying, of course. Easier to supervise that way; nothing can take place behind his back. Too many stories of returning from the Mall with one family in excess and another minus one. (Only even exchanges are desired.) The father bobs up and down to keep his passenger amused, content. Hear the responsive gurgling: index of success. In front of him in

MARY CAPONEGRO

line a mother struggles with her first-grader who insists on one more game, another toy, more time to look around. All parents know that shopping only between kids is ideal but sometimes just not feasible. And conscientious parents who aim for early Christmas shopping are inevitably thwarted. The item they pluck from the shelf will very likely have, at home, a longer shelf-life than the child for whom they're buying it.

"It's been years since I rocked a baby in my arms," the mother says, to her surprise, out loud, as she observes the father/baby interaction. Already her daughter's getting nervous— she thought she'd get at least a week out of this cushy situation. Even the baby seems to see what's coming. "Funny," muses Father, "I was just wondering how it would be when junior here is on his feet and filled with speech and toilet-trained and . . ."—cuts himself off—"of course, I'll never get that far . . . unless by some coincidence he returns to me years from now, but with so many in between, how could one recognize . . . ? I don't know that it's ever happened, have you ever heard . . . ?"

Impulsively, she interrupts his incoherent rumination, looks him urgently in the eye, angling her head ever so slightly toward her collateral. Into his ear she whispers, "Shall we just do it? Right here? Now?" The girl, who doesn't need to overhear to sense that something is amiss, blurts out, "Hey, what's going on? I'll find my own parents, thank you!" as the child-sack is lifted over her new father's head onto the former mother's shoulders, and the girl's hand is transferred to his with no salespersons or customers the wiser. "If you're really that unhappy, kaitlin, ditch him in the parking lot. Watch out for cars, though," she calls out as she hastens away with her new charge. "Hey, what about my stuff?" "Now that, dear, is a stupid question."

⌒ XVIII ⌒

But shopping for candy breeds almost as much anxiety as shopping for toys because the most alarming evening for the rents is Halloween, a sanctioned cruising holiday—its emblem the shameless glance over the shoulder of the candy giver to assess his, her, or their abode's interior. The gumdrops, candycorns, mars bars and hershey's kisses are excuses, ruses, confectionary decoys; in other words, for trick-or-treat, read, take-me-in. This method furnishes a process of elimination far more expedient than without these glimpses; children can cross off the list a house in which they may have otherwise had to spend an entire day!

Will they open up the door for you and leave it propped? That's what you wonder, what you hope. The trouble is that then it's open for the next kid in line as well, with his scary mask or silly hat that fools no one, open for the veritable assembly line of pirates and goblins and witches and wolves, ghosts, skeletons and princesses and ladies of the evening. Go ahead. Hold out your gaping candy bag. Wear your emptiness on your sleeve. For isn't this just a stylized version of your lives? Ding and you're here, dong and the next one arrives to take your place, grabs a handful of candy, and moves on. So tiresome, so inconsolably predictable, so much so that you wonder if it might be better never to have been born.

XIX

Fire, fire, everywhere. The red truck she hoped for under the tree, bright as a lipstick, is now life-size and multiplied, as the men in slickers and helmets aim their hoses everywhere that says flame. To you it's one big birthday cake that blazes forth the sum of all collective child years. A conflagration composed of a million candles standing for an exponential lie, or an incendiary veil both cloaking and exposing annihilation. Even the ghosts that congregate this night in the village cemetery have something more concrete than any kid; they have dates etched in stone, a tomb to anchor them like a steady wrist tied to a recalcitrant rising balloon.

No matter. The funny hoses blow with water instead of breath, but the party's over anyway. It's just for kicks, each year, a kind of punctuation to the antics of the night before. "It says that we mean business," jen proclaims. "A statement: we're in charge," adds mike. "A little acting out is all." That's tim's interpretation, added to by tom: "You know, against routine." "In any case," debbie concludes, "we always make sure they remember All Saints' Day." "All Souls'," corrects heather. "All kids," the sweating fireman says, "should be sent back to where they came from." Then back to normal. Everybody scramble. Pick a new house.

XX

How mortifying when, as you gather round the tube, *THE FATING GAME* comes on. Is it already seven-thirty? The show is on hiatus, they are playing reruns, and who should one of the three couples behind the partition be but—yes, you guessed—your current parents! Oh, the shame! For whom? You? Them? They turn the sound off furtively as soon as the gawky blonde girl asks the opening question. Thus the young contestant who has her way with them communicates only motion after her mouth inquires coyly, "What would you consider the ideal family evening at home?"

Your parents are playing every card they've got; you see it in their faces, even in the few pans allotted by the camera among the other couples competing. You feel how much they want to take her home and at the same time you feel, somehow, soiled. They scan your eyes for permission to turn it off—it's you who hold the magic wand—in order to let your mutual humiliation find surcease, as if they feared your very presence in their living room were rendered null and void by its convergence with the drama implicit behind the scenes, or between the lines, as it were, of the screen. Thus the ideal evening at home, ostensibly come true for them, through you, turns out to be—through the exposure of their *wishing* it, or more correctly, having wished—a travesty.

"Oh hey," you say, "who are we kidding anyway? Nobody's pure in this. We've all already been around the block." (Later their eyes stare through the picture window as if to itemize their neighbors.) "I'll admit I've sat on other sofas, just as other kids have sat here. So what? The stuff on TV or at the Bar or Park or Mall—what difference does it make? We're all out hustling in our way. Don't sweat it, folks. Don't take it personally. I won't."

MARY CAPONEGRO

XXI

What is it about you anyway? Somehow you're demographically the perfect child: just the right mix of goofy and sweet, courteous, smart-ass, precocious, sensitive, and edging with endearing awkwardness toward adolescence. You don't threaten, neither do you bore; the many parents you have sampled seem engaged by you. Maybe it's because you're not as put-off by the corny stuff as your peers are. The birth-certificate ritual, for example. When they leave the xerox on the coffee table with a fresh bottle of white-out, you don't see the harm in humoring them by letting your name lie upon the line provided, for the night or fortnight you lie in the bed upstairs (although increasingly you feel it a matter of integrity to leave the space at *date* unfilled). Sometimes you'd like a moment to reflect amid the cumulative onslaught of embrace. You know how fortunate you are, but all the overwhelming change . . . and yet a moment's contemplation would be enough to send you reeling into the void, and you can't afford right now to calculate the relative merits of never having been born.

XXII

Are they in the drawer? Under the bed? Inside the under-bed storage unit? In the farthest corner of the closet floor or way back on the closet shelf? Under the stereo? Where has your predecessor hidden her or his stash? No, not under the pillow; anyone could find them there. Every child, whether genius or dork, confident, awkward, or arrogant, participates unanimously in one particular rite of passage, which evolves into routine. She or he must have been a genius, to hide them so well. And you'd best be one yourself, to find them. For child's sake, isn't there even one issue? Maybe the toy chest? Yes! Oh damn! To go through all that searching and discover *PLAYMOM!* This confirms, a toddler was your predecessor. The cleavage contest issue; give me strength, you groan. It's embarrassing is what it is, to be reminded of your earliest inexperienced years. Memory can no longer supply to you the plethora of tastes you acquired, each mother's milk a new delicacy, some sweeter, some thicker, some richer, all whole-some, all hitting the spot, all right on the money (Oh Breast!) when you possessed a crude articulation that was itself volition: Mama, Mama, and it swelled for you, your wails its reveille; even before your eyes could see that far you'd sense it rise to you, your call, the nipple puckering in tandem with your tiny lips.

Alas, you're past that now, it's all outgrown; you want as any self-respecting adolescent does, the clothed centerfold for ages three and up. You'd recognize it instantly, the issue of *PLAYRENT* you most prize, with both parents standing regally, arms out-stretched, their eyes imploring you. It's the magazine that features words as well, articles and interviews on how to manage the frantic pace and how to keep your cool, although no article ever addresses that white noise of evaluating whether it would be bet-ter never to have been born.

Even now you see the father's strong white teeth, gleaming with a luster greater than all cumulative color. His shoulders, were they hunched or straight? mike and tim and tom and jeff all say straight shoulders in a dad is key, is primary, but hell,

MARY CAPONEGRO

maybe the slouching guy just had a bad day. Who wants to pose for this shit anyway? Debates among your friends abound: are the posers proud to set the standard? Or desperate since they can't find a connection any other way than putting themselves— standing in, as it were, for their toys—on display?

The smiles invariably get the most attention. The mouth is scrutinized for evidence of earnestness or ambivalence. Posture is a high priority as well. Stooped shoulders, slouching: notorious signs of weariness, the side effects of carrying too many aquariums. The judgments are for the most part instant and irrevocable. One child learns from another how to fashion them and levy them. Hours are spent distinguishing a genuine from a fake. See the seemingly flawless curve of that mouth with its perfect proportion of upper to lower lip, enhanced by dimples, no less; it makes an irresistible affectionate smile.

Now, imagine that smile greeting you each morning. You do, over and over, imagine it, and achieve a species of catharsis in this fashion; in fact you would not dare disclose to tim and tom how fervently you carry in your mind the image of that tender beckoning crescent, a haven you drift toward in moments of distress or inattention or confusion. You remember your shock and feeling of betrayal when tom informed you that those images were not entirely authentic. "It's doctored," was the way jeff put it. Ever since that incident, your friends have lost no opportunity to assess your progress, test your powers of discernment. Each time you're taken with an image, each time you skate on the periphery of reverie, they jerk you back to earth: "Can't you tell it's airbrushing?" And if you hesitate a second, the *nya-nya-nya-nya-nyaa-nyaa* commences: "howie doesn't get it; howie doesn't get it!"

"Well what, in that case," you protest—refusing to capitulate or mimic their immaturity—"is wishing for? Why have these lures at all? Is it considered consolation, when the postures, when the parents' very bearing is leading us toward what can never be attained? I mean, for rents' sake, why stock the bait if all the fish are fake?"

"Get real, howard," debbie says. "Yeah, he's real," chimes in tim, "a real party pooper." "You know, I just don't give a toy," says jeff, exasperated. "Will everyone shut up so I can read?" "You call this reading?" megan challenges. "It's howie's house, remember?" mike interjects to your relief. "He asked us over. Don't give him such a hard time."

And they comply, though inadvertently, mutating from abusive to dismissive to preoccupied. jeff and jen and debbie eventually glaze over in front of the October issue. You know the image: ingeniously simple: a man and woman's face in profile with a seductive child-sized space between them. They'll hover over it for hours. Meanwhile, tim and tom are ticked off by the farm scene in the month before. "Give me a break, what do they take us for?" one asks the other. "They've got some nerve to print this! . . . it's so . . . fakey."

And indeed, they have a point; a lapse in judgment may be the best explanation for the close-up of a father's hand around a child's around the udder of a cow, conveying the jubilant, triumphant sensation of the squeeze. Strange though, to see an actual child explicitly included. "megan, isn't that illegal?" you call over. Incensed, they tear it out and toss it in the trash.

As for RENTS' HOUSE, at one time, censors allowed only the exteriors to be displayed, leaving inside to the imagination. All viewers had abundant two-dimensional access to wood, stucco, brick, or cobblestone. But now, of course, interiors are standard fare, nothing too precious for the page, even the fluffy canopy bed that jeff says is sissy stuff. You're inclined to agree, as it reminds you of the fabric awning vigilantly shading the precious hairless noggin of the itty-bitty one inside his imported collapsible stroller. For child's sake, his whole head's a bald spot. What's so adorable?

But the question on every kid's mind, no matter what the season, is what will be featured this month? You've placed a bet with mike that this time it will be the king-size bathroom with shower-massager and jacuzzi, three heads bobbing above the foam, two fully articulated in their features but one vacant oval to FILL IN THE BLANK of, and every child cuts his or her little photo-face and pastes it to the vacant space, even if another child's head got there first.

"But once you get there," proposes debbie, "once you're there a week? Whose hot tub is it gonna be?" "Oh, come on," heather says. "They know if they turn off the jets, you blow the joint. What parent will dare say, 'OK, jacuzzi is off-limits now'?" "It's all irrelevant," you intervene, "since no one stays a week. Well, almost no one." "You've got a point there, howard." Your banal discussion is interrupted by tim and tom shouting, in stereo, at all of you to come look. "megan fished the farm scene out of the trash! megan fished the farm scene out of the tra-ash! Look, she's getting off on it!" Again, you feel compelled to clarify, "She's checking it because I asked her if it was illegal to use a kid like that, remember?" tom won't relent. "Yeah, sure, howard. Is that why she's crying then?" megan tries to shield her face but the tear has already been perceived. Caught in the act of wishing: the worst vulnerability to suffer amid peers. "megan's wishing! megan's wishing! Off a jerky picture!"

"So what's the use of wishing then?" you carry on, running interference in the hope of mitigating megan's torture, although your question is, as ever, genuine, not at all rhetorical despite its form, and yet it might as well be, for the lack of response. Accept that there's no answer here. Nor is there answer to the larger question that pervades your private meditations. Those to whom you sometimes wake cannot abide to contemplate the answer either, because they stand as alternate, thus seek instinctively to block your option of not being born, and of imagining not being born.

XXIII

As if there weren't enough to make one anxious, you have to be alert to a signal in yourself that it is time. You must eventually step over to the other side. You will be required to find, quickly, a teammate and to look through the list of vacant houses and to accrue the enormous expenses of soliciting the class of individuals

MARY CAPONEGRO

who until yesterday would have included you. It will be particularly awkward if it happens before, say, megan's, mike's and jeff's and debbie's change; they'll look across the park at you as if you were a traitor or a square, as if these transmutations were within a person's power to schedule, but soon enough, soon enough, you'll find them in the house next door, and even in competition. Perhaps megan would team up with you, and if not she, heather? It's not as if there's any choice in it. Whoever is available will show up in the kitchen or the basement or the bath. There's no time for discriminating in these partnerships when all your energy is taken up in trying to score. And if you execute a smooth transition and make a seamless team, then all the better, to facilitate your being chosen. No manual is required, or rather, none is offered. Just sign the lease. Amass and divvy up the goods. That's all you'll have to do.

It should be better. At last the weight of childhood brooding will be lifted. The stress of scoring prime child cannot help but tax you less than your habitual concerns. Once maturation brings you to the fence's other side, you might well shed the questioning, might leave your skepticism at the door, since when you're hustling, surely you cannot afford to ponder whether it were better never to be born.

Accept your lot, get on with it, stiff upper lip, and don't indulge yourself, except, for child's sake, i.e.: at TOYS-Q-US. "How adolescent!" jeff, mike, debbie, heather, tim, and tom will eventually complain if you submit for discussion an existential dilemma. "I don't remember ever wondering that," they'll insist. "And isn't that irrelevant? Besides, howard, it's almost dark. Dig up some bat-teries. Clean out this old aquarium! Parade's about to start. For rents' sake, howie, don't slouch!"

The prospect alone is enough to send you pouring over *RENTS' HOUSE,* even *PLAYMOM,* as a tonic, no, a life-preserver. There is a guaranteed release in the familiar arc that starts at stimulation and concludes with soothing. What's your pleasure? Which one will it be? No hesitation: the close-up sequence of a tender wav-ing hand behind a windowpane, the glass so clear. Five glossy pages; they fold out almost like a flip book to ensure you can cre-ate the motion in your mind, like a pendulum that speeds and slows according to your needs, goes right to left and back again, for as long as you desire. You trace the life-lines in the palm with your own fingertip, then, knowing privacy is for the moment assured, your tongue.

You have no idea how to read a palm or prophesy the future, but you sense if this were actual flesh before your eyes right now, it might somehow reveal the past. You might be able—through a scrutiny of the uniquely etched configuration, its rivulets and deltas, its forked or braided paths—to glean essen-tial information: were you born and were you better never born?

"Why won't you come out of your room tonight, howard?"

You can't confess, "to delay as long as possible becoming you."

⌒ XXIV ⌒

Carpe diem. Something that the teacher said, in passing, lodged inside your head. If whatever this has been is soon to be surrendered, or transformed, make the most of it. And what better opportunity than the most anxious day of the year? The electricity in the air on this late December morning is not to be attributed exclusively to the strings of lights twined over branches, hedges, houses, doorways. No household is exempt from this ritual: the culmination, in a sense, of everyday giving.

Keeping up with the Joneses is all the more the order of this day, and on this day particularly, a daunting agenda. In many houses, ladders are set up to permit children access to the piles of presents reaching as high as the star on the tree's tippy-top, and it is not unusual for children to wave to each other through the house's highest windows, from their respective perches, when parents are distracted. Unwrapping is precarious and exhausting; children whose agility has been facilitated by sports participation and informal athletic activities now benefit. Autumn gym classes at school traditionally devote one session per week to the game of "reach for the star," during which the basketball hoop is supplanted by a facsimile of what will cap the tree on Christmas Eve. The trampoline is employed for developing height and balance. Shop classes occasionally implement student suggestions to design a ladder with padded rungs.

It is considered common courtesy to linger over every gift, regardless of their number and regardless of the unremarkable nature of the practice of receiving. Today is distinct from other days only in that a layer of surprise surrounds each present, and in that these objects are guaranteed hot-off-the-shelf, i.e.: not yet used: one hundred percent NEW.

That distinction merits fawning over, does it not? You ooohh and aahhh on cue and daintily as possible remove, then fold the pretty crinkly paper while suspended from the chandelier or sky-light, or while clinging to the ladder's second-highest rung, or else thrusting out your arms from an excavated pit within the moun-tainous conglomerate, all the while taking care not to displace ornaments or lose your concentration—or worse yet, balance—due to an unsuppressible sneeze. If only the tinsel (whose inter-minable meticulous dissemination gave you a headache in the first place) did not tickle so. Even if it wasn't this tree in this house whose decoration included your participation, it was one just like it.

No matter. This is where you spent the much-coveted night of Christmas Eve. It was not snow that woke you, nor the shadow of an obese, bearded man, nor the muffled percussion of his primitive transport across the roof. Pretend for them (i.e., your parents) it was excitement that inspired you to rise at dawn, rather than the literal alarm clock in your heart or head. Pretend, again for them, that you would be delighted to attend a post-toy-getting service—if this is their custom—in that special breed of house whose stained glass and distinctively set table has yet to be exposed in RENTS' HOUSE Don't let on that even the awkward, chipped clay figurines, conspicuously NOT new, nestled under the burdened pine tree's lowest branch, make you uneasy. You notice

MARY CAPONEGRO

that their little wooden house, although it has a sort of roof, is open-faced: a gallery of simplicity. It's like a farm too, though you don't know what the animals are really doing there. The donkey, for example, seems too close a relative of the image on which you pin the tail at other parties. As for the humans, the kings seem ostentatiously archaic, and the man and woman equally unconvincing in their humility. Come on, who lives like that?

Thanks to megan, you detect the oxymoron. Thanks to you, you recognize it as contrived. Meanwhile, the baby lying complacent on his ersatz straw commands—does it surprise you?—everyone's attention. You've heard of him yourself, seen him somewhere. Or maybe everywhere. He didn't come from TOYS-Y-US, although almost every other object on the floor did, and even now encroaches upon his trademark village. The whole scene reinforces only your uncertainty as to whether he, if able to foresee the hyperbolic distortions in the legacy of frankincense and myrrh, would ever have elected to be born.

His story is so strange. Did it create this day, or did this day create him? The lucky lamb; at least he has a narrative of being born. For child's sake, time is split along the seam of his supposed birth. He is the fundament for all the history you learn in school, and lots of people think he isn't even real. Go figure!

Yet there his little manger sits, wedged between two segments of conveniently initialed time, for what would otherwise provide a reference? How would one demarcate the condition of never having been born? What acronym could do it justice, or for that matter, not glut the tongue with consonants? B.N.B.?

A.N.B.? P.N.B.? Before or after or perhaps or better never born? Or would an image be more accurate? A volleyball suspended in glorious momentary spin—perhaps its blur alone to represent this modest, suspect fulcrum for an oblivious, compulsive, turning earth. All time leads up to or away from him, and by extension to the props of this most familiar stage set. How right it seems, though corny, that the kings are bearing gifts—even if one has a gouge in it—this baby's power is no secret.

He's got it made. Even those who don't buy him acknowledge him; they buy around him, and indirectly, at least celebrate him. The music pumped into the Mall during holiday season would be full of holes without his name, holes to take the place of the implicit wounds that make him, even prior to receiving them, a star. "What is your deal?" you want to shout at him. "You've got it both ways! You're on the top; you're at the base. A bleating sheep, a shining star, an oozing wound!

"You lucky duck, you schmuck, you superhero! You don't even need a cape, your blazing insignia worn across your skin, ensuring you will never wake from nightmares dubbed a goose. You play it every way. You've got your cake, they eat out of your hand, they lick your wounds, your heart's a flaming candle dripping wax, they spit at you to try to blow it out, and yet they bow to you as well, they try to rip you from the picture only to find you leave a big, fat hole."

He's got a story any kid would be sent home a liar for telling, but somehow this big baby stands for what is brave and true. The common sense prized by parents suggests he would have better missed his grand debut as THE SCAPEGOAT, THE PINNED DONKEY, THE SLAUGHTERED LAMB, but whoever wrote his script made sure that no one could conceive of his not being born. After all, who needs a house when his story is completely furnished? Who needs a parent when his father is built-in? Why bother envying a baby when you stay one for two thousand years?

For child's sake, who can stand to think about it? (If only you could have a story too, a story that compelling, straining credibility yet curiously persuasive.) It makes your head swim. Makes your heart race. Just push that crèche way back against the trunk, why don't you? Let it lie under the harmless paper avalanche until tomorrow, or twelve days from now, or until you too can conjure up a story that would, by ingenious or outrageous means, arrest your chronic visitation to the house of never being born.

OTHER STORY COLLECTIONS
BY MARY CAPONEGRO

COLOPHON

The Complexities of Intimacy was designed at Coffee House Press
in the Warehouse District of downtown Minneapolis.
The text is set in Bembo.

The coffee house of seventeenth-century England was a place of fellowship where ideas could be freely exchanged. The coffee house of 1950s America was a place of refuge and of tremendous literary energy. At the turn of our latest century, coffee house culture abounds at corner shops and on-line. We hope this spirit welcomes our readers into the pages of Coffee House Press books.

TITLES BY COFFEE HOUSE PRESS

Prayers of an Accidental Nature, short stories by Debra Di Blasi. "Di Blasi's themes of sexual obsession, physical beauty and lost love ignite this notable effort to define the perils of intimacy." —PUBLISHERS WEEKLY
$13.95, PAPER, 1-56689-083-7.

Our Sometime Sister, a novel by Norah Labiner. "Combines lively storytelling with Labiner's unique skill at conveying psychological depth. . . . Equally important to her is the deft mix of cultural references, from old TV shows to Shakespeare's Hamlet." —UTNE READER
$15.95, PAPER, 1-55689-095-0 / $22.95, CLOTH, 1-55689-072-1.

Portrait of the Walrus by a Young Artist, a novel by Laurie Foos. "A mad tale of a mad genius, by a young author who may be a genius herself. . . . Brilliant, fresh, and remarkable: one of the few works of recent years in which brave original-ity is sustained by genuine skill." —KIRKUS REVIEWS
$19.95, CLOTH, 1-56689-057-8.

The Song of Percival Peacock, a novel by Russell Edson. "If Henry Miller had written *Alice in Wonderland,* he may have come up with something like Edson's first work of extended fiction." —CAPITOL TIMES
$11.95, PAPER, 1-56689-002-0.

good books are brewing
at coffeehousepress.org

"Outside of a dog
a book is man's best friend.
Inside of a dog
it's too hard to read."

—GROUCHO MARX